Hex Vet

Witches in Training

kaboom!™

ROSS RICHIE...CEO & Founder
JOY HUFFMAN...CFO
MATT GAGNON......................................Editor-in-Chief
FILIP SABLIK.........................President, Publishing & Marketing
STEPHEN CHRISTY.........................President, Development
LANCE KREITER.........Vice President, Licensing & Merchandising
PHIL BARBARO.........Vice President, Finance & Human Resources
ARUNE SINGH..............Vice President, Marketing
BRYCE CARLSON.....Vice President, Editorial & Creative Strategy
SCOTT NEWMAN..............................Manager, Production Design
KATE HENNING...Manager, Operations
SPENCER SIMPSON...Manager, Sales
SIERRA HAHN...Executive Editor
JEANINE SCHAEFER.....................................Executive Editor
DAFNA PLEBAN..Senior Editor
SHANNON WATTERS...Senior Editor
ERIC HARBURN...Senior Editor
WHITNEY LEOPARD...Editor
CAMERON CHITTOCK..Editor
CHRIS ROSA...Editor
MATTHEW LEVINE

SOPHIE PHILIPS-ROBERTS..............................Assistant Editor
GAVIN GRONENTHAL...Assistant Editor
MICHAEL MOCCIO..Assistant Editor
AMANDA LaFRANCO.......................................Executive Assistant
JILLIAN CRAB..Design Coordinator
MICHELLE ANKLEY.......................................Design Coordinator
KARA LEOPARD...Production Designer
MARIE KRUPINA.......................................Production Designer
GRACE PARK................................Production Design Assistant
CHELSEA ROBERTS....................Production Design Assistant
SAMANTHA KNAPP....................Production Design Assistant
ELIZABETH LOUGHRIDGE..................Accounting Coordinator
STEPHANIE HOCUTT..................Social Media Coordinator
JOSÉ MEZA...Event Coordinator
HOLLY AITCHISON.............................Operations Coordinator
MEGAN CHRISTOPHER...........................Operations Assistant
RODRIGO HERNANDEZ..............................Mailroom Assistant
MORGAN PERRY..........Direct Market Representative
CAT O'GRADY..Marketing Assistant
BREANNA SARPY...Executive Assistant

HEX VET: WITCHES IN TRAINING, December 2018. Published by KaBOOM!, a division of Boom Entertainment, Inc. Hex Vet is ™ & © 2018 Sam Davies. All rights reserved. KaBOOM!™ and the KaBOOM! logo are trademarks of Boom Entertainment, Inc., registered in various countries and categories. All characters, events, and/or institutions depicted herein are fictional. Any similarity between any of the names, characters, persons, events, and/or institutions in this publication to actual names, characters, and persons, whether living or dead, events, and/or institutions is unintended and purely coincidental. KaBOOM! does not read or accept unsolicited submissions of ideas, stories, or artwork.

For information regarding the CPSIA on this printed material, call: (203) 595-3636 and provide reference #RICH – 828620.

BOOM! Studios, 5670 Wilshire Boulevard, Suite 400, Los Angeles, CA 90036-5679. Printed in USA. First Printing.

ISBN: 978-1-68415-288-9, eISBN: 978-1-64144-127-8

Scholastic Edition:
ISBN: 978-1-68415-414-2

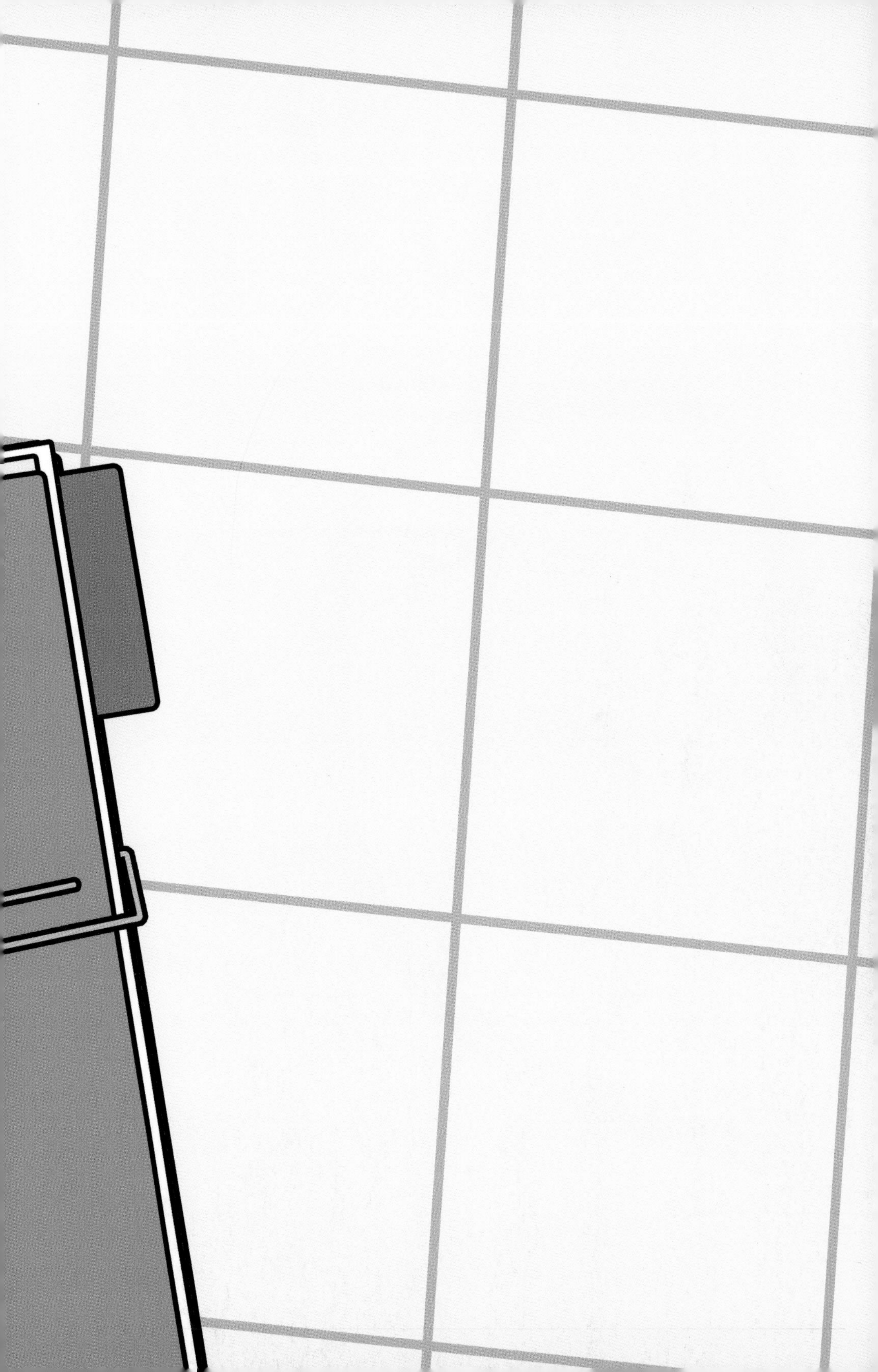

Hex Vet™

Witches in Training

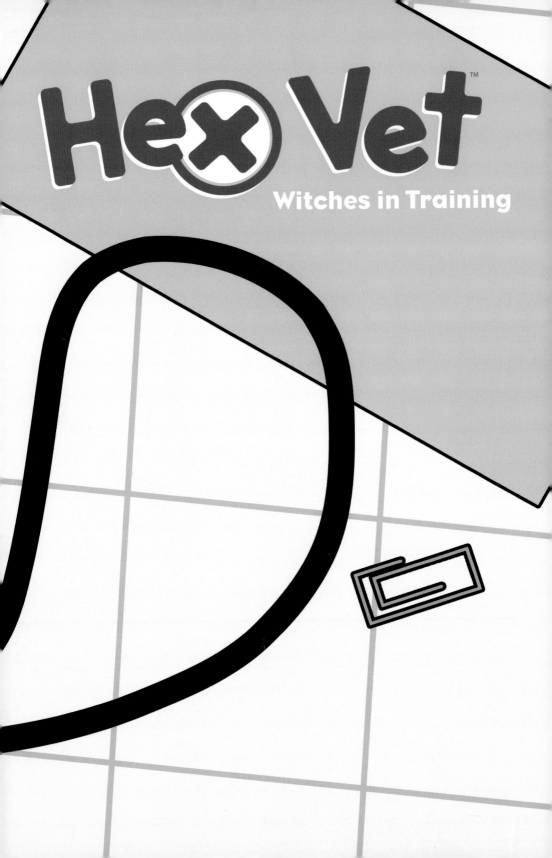

Written & Illustrated by
Sam Davies

Letters by
Mike Fiorentino

Cover by
Sam Davies

Designer
Kara Leopard

Editor
Whitney Leopard

Welcome to Willows Whisper Veterinary Practice

Meet our team:

Dr. Cornelia Talon
Head Veterinary Witch,
High Society of Sorcerer's
with honours.

Nurse Ariel Chantsworth
Registered veterinary Witch,
head of administration.

Meet the trainees:

Clarion Wellspring

Annette Artifice

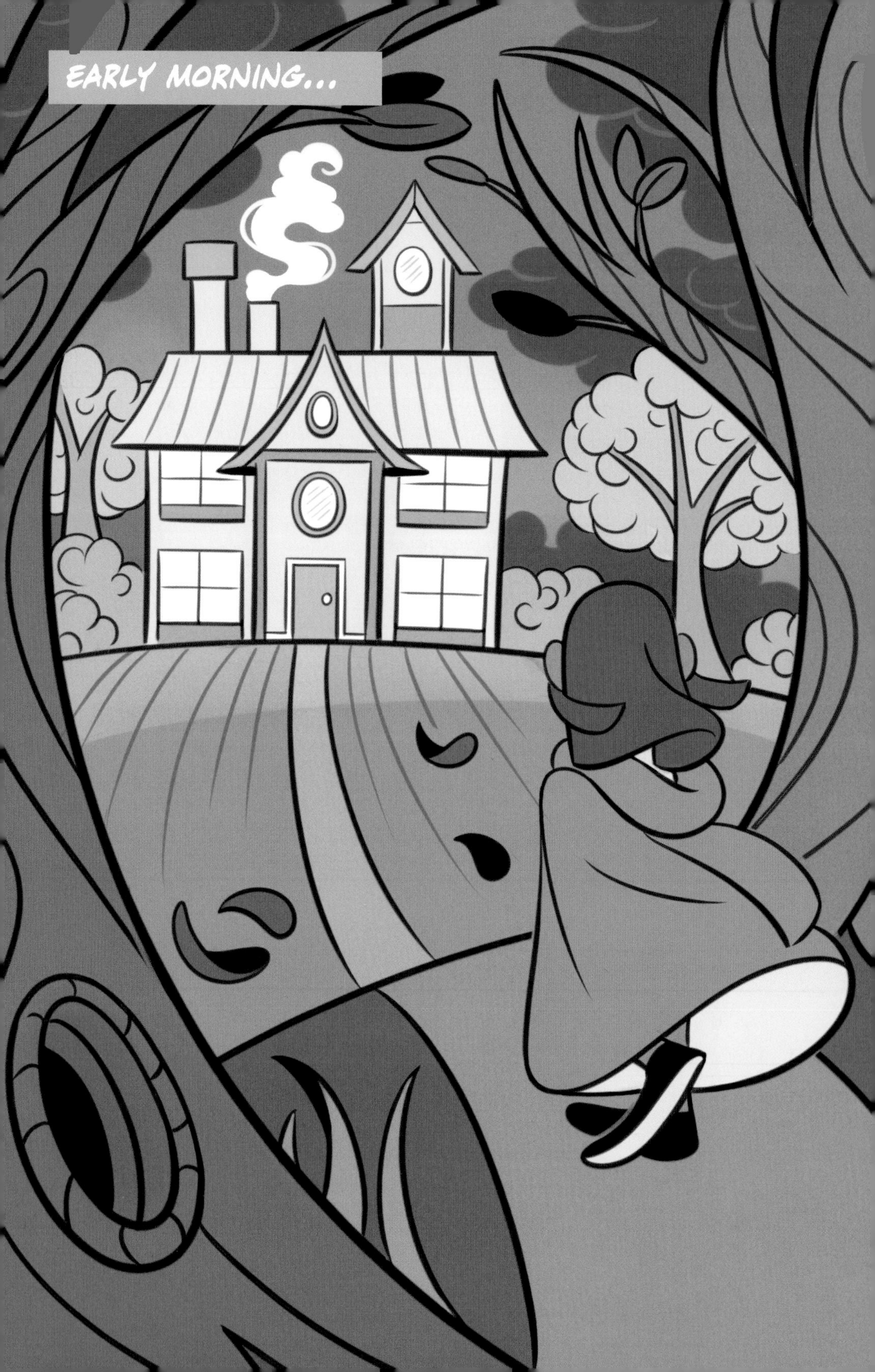
EARLY MORNING...

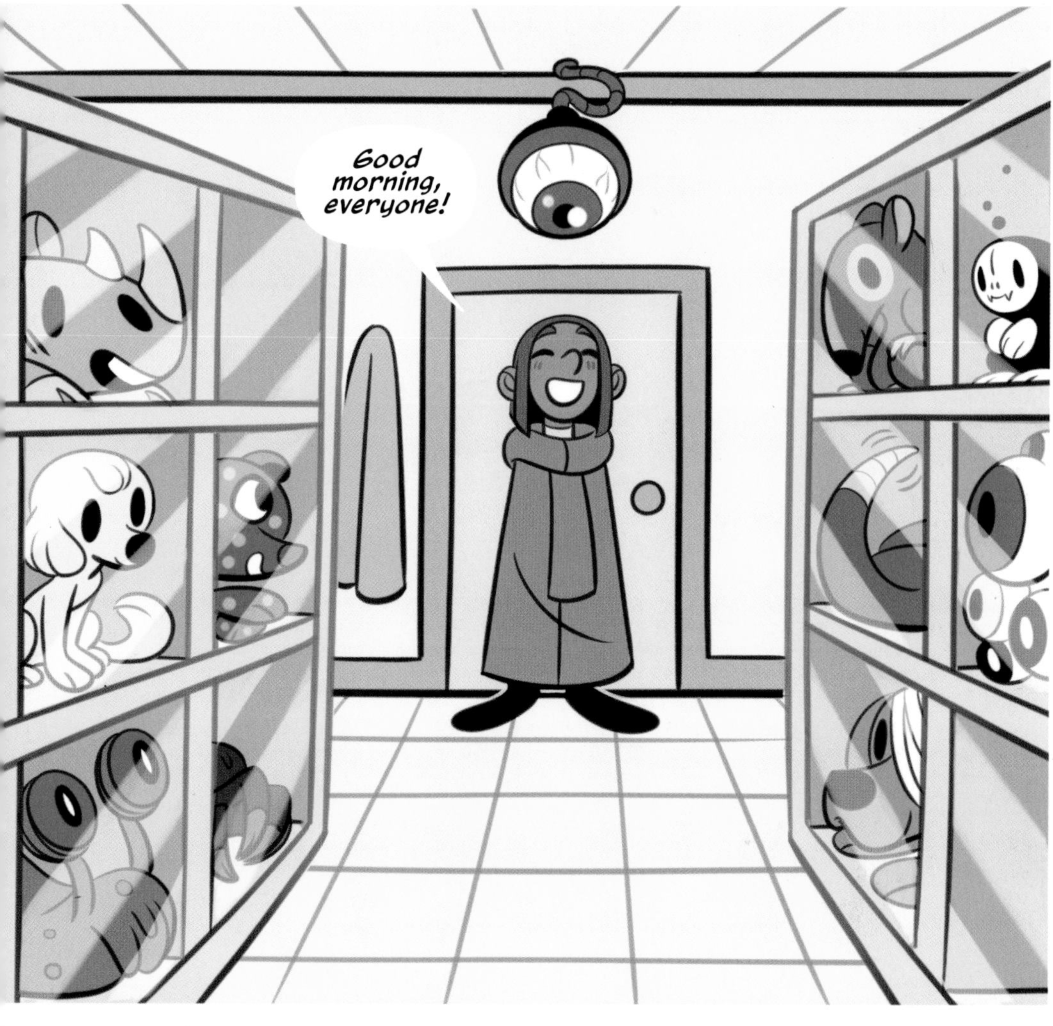
Good morning, everyone!

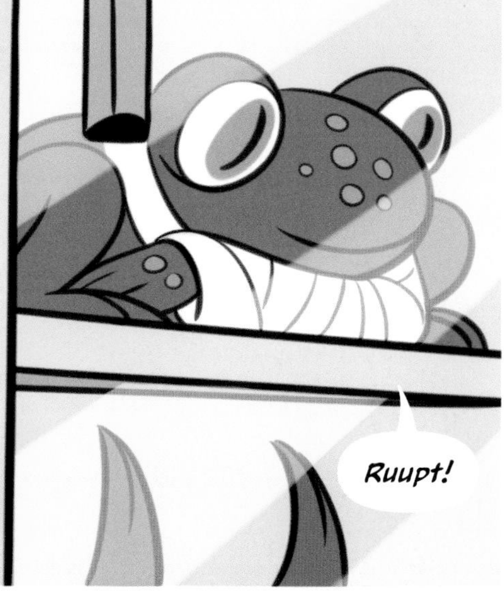
Ruupt!

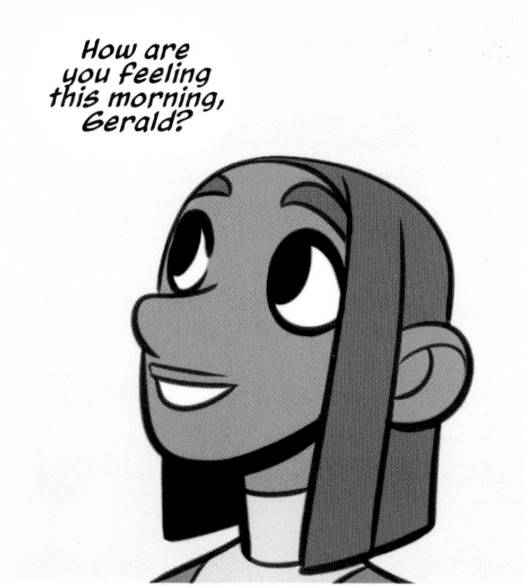
How are you feeling this morning, Gerald?

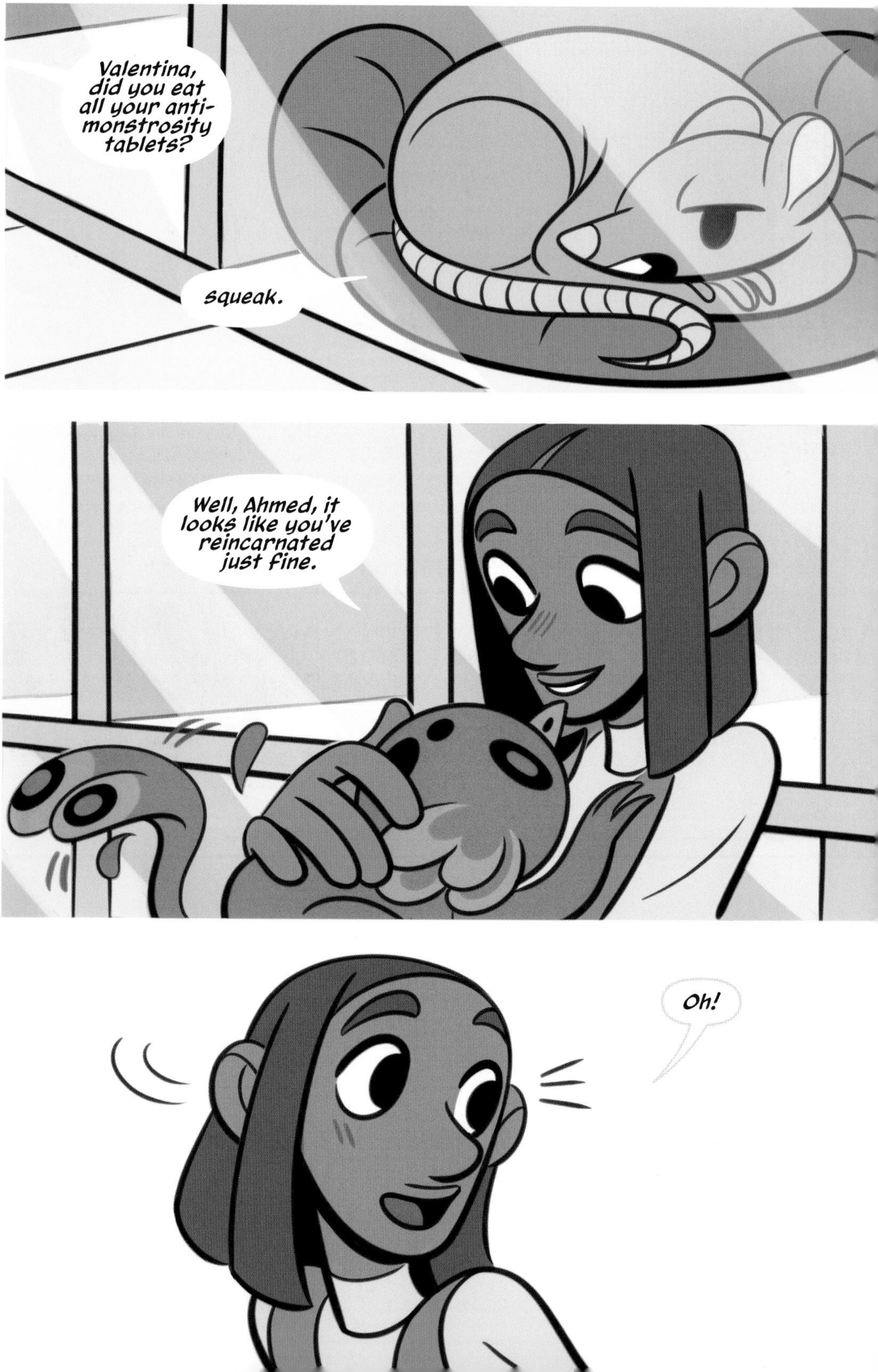
Valentina, did you eat all your anti-monstrosity tablets?
squeak.
Well, Ahmed, it looks like you've reincarnated just fine.
Oh!

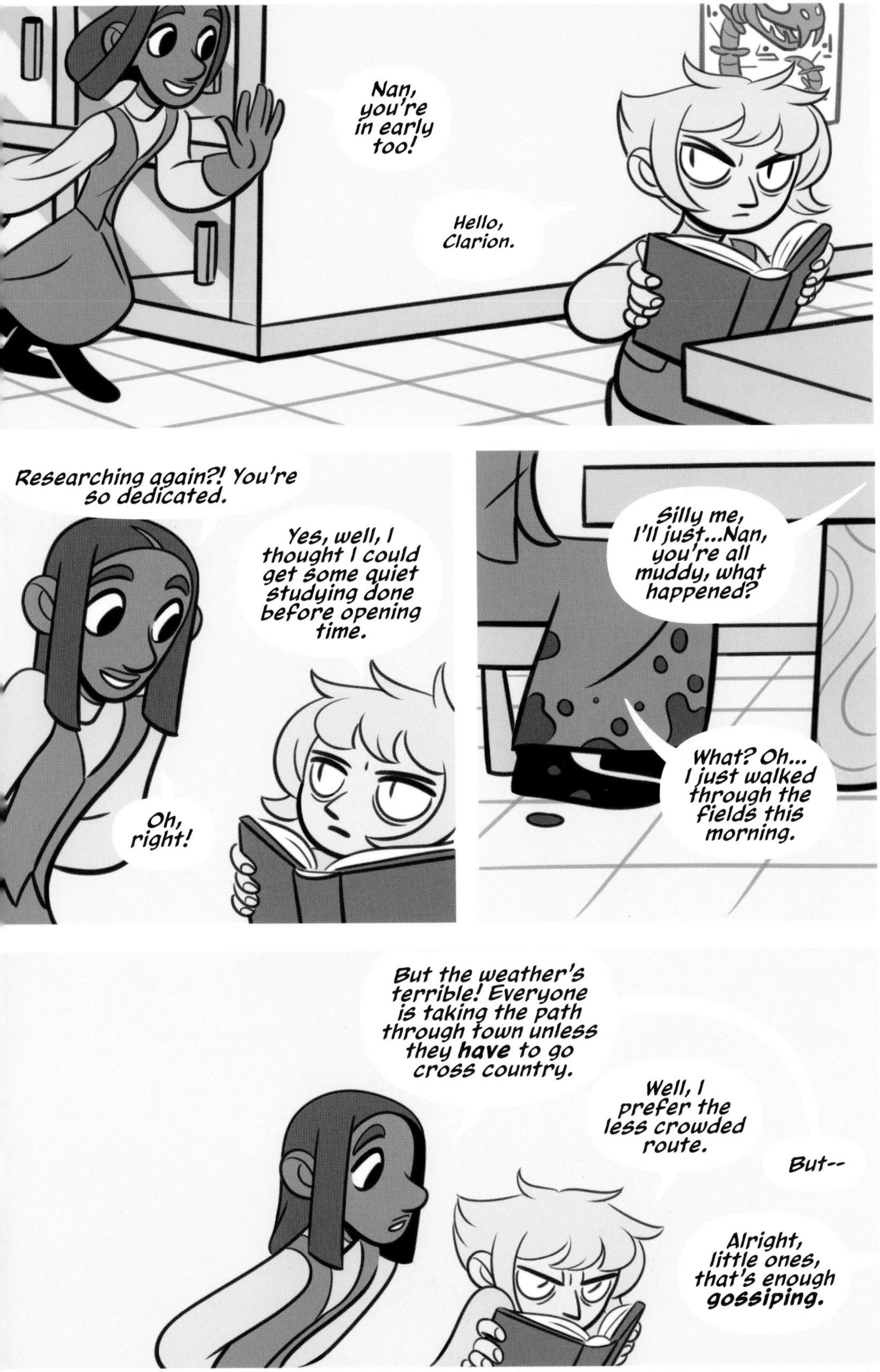
Nan, you're in early too!
Hello, Clarion.
Researching again?! You're so dedicated.
Yes, well, I thought I could get some quiet studying done before opening time.
Oh, right!
Silly me, I'll just...Nan, you're all muddy, what happened?
What? Oh... I just walked through the fields this morning.
But the weather's terrible! Everyone is taking the path through town unless they **have** to go cross country.
Well, I prefer the less crowded route.
But--
Alright, little ones, that's enough **gossiping.**

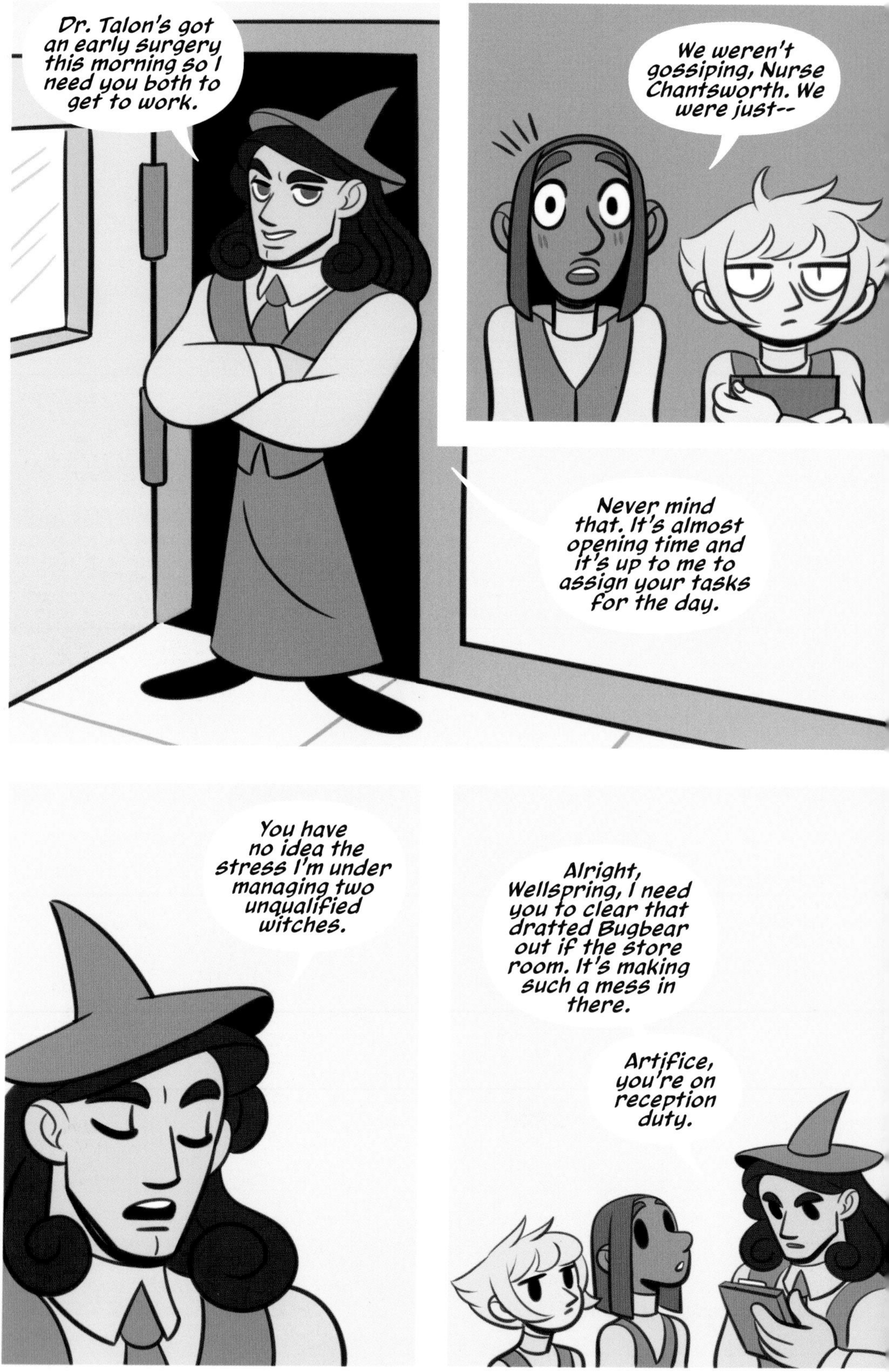
Dr. Talon's got an early surgery this morning so I need you both to get to work.
We weren't gossiping, Nurse Chantsworth. We were just--
Never mind that. It's almost opening time and it's up to me to assign your tasks for the day.
You have no idea the stress I'm under managing two unqualified witches.
Alright, Wellspring, I need you to clear that dratted Bugbear out if the store room. It's making such a mess in there.
Artifice, you're on reception duty.

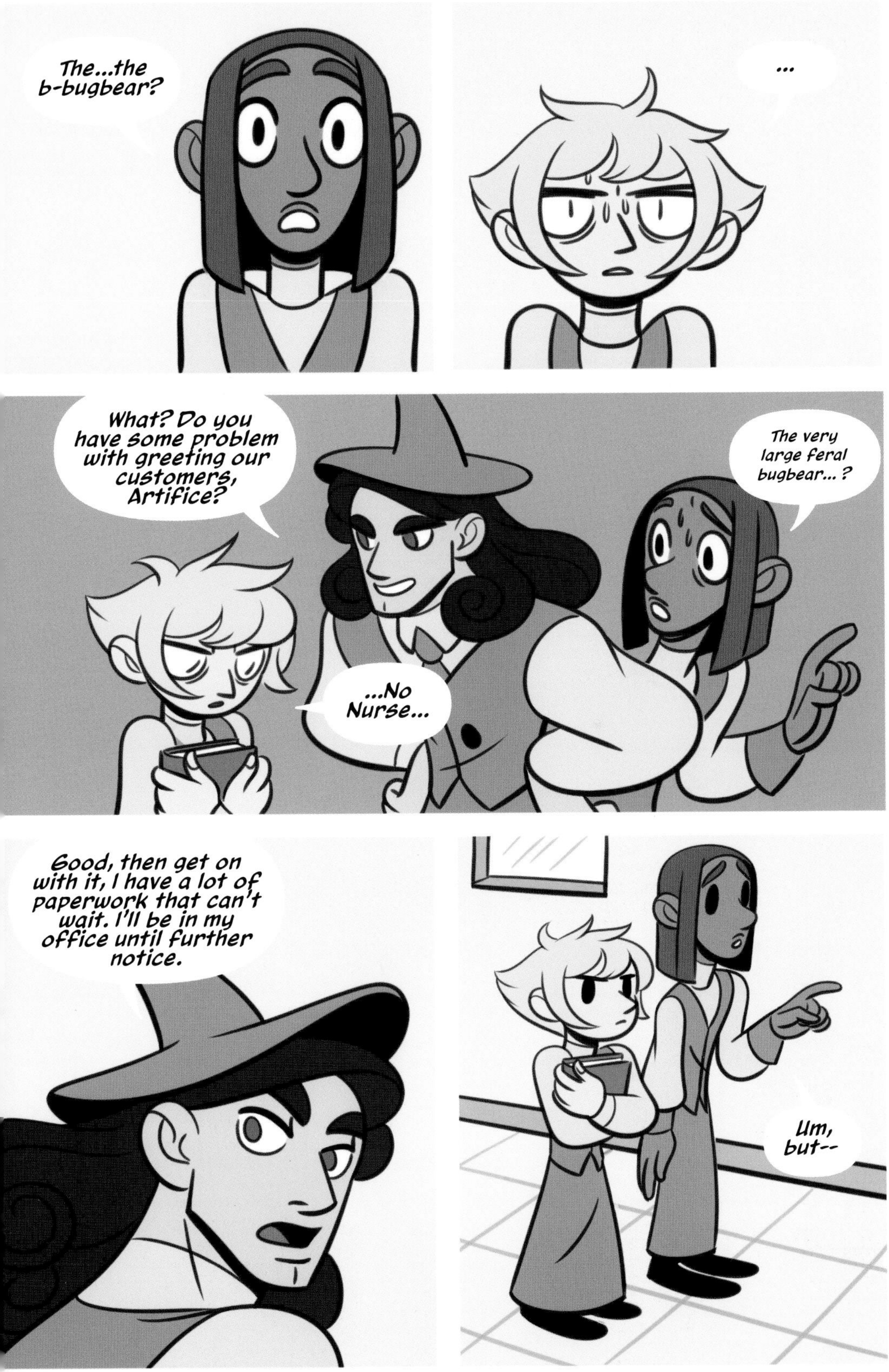
The...the b-bugbear?
...
What? Do you have some problem with greeting our customers, Artifice?
The very large feral bugbear...?
...No Nurse...
Good, then get on with it, I have a lot of paperwork that can't wait. I'll be in my office until further notice.
Um, but--

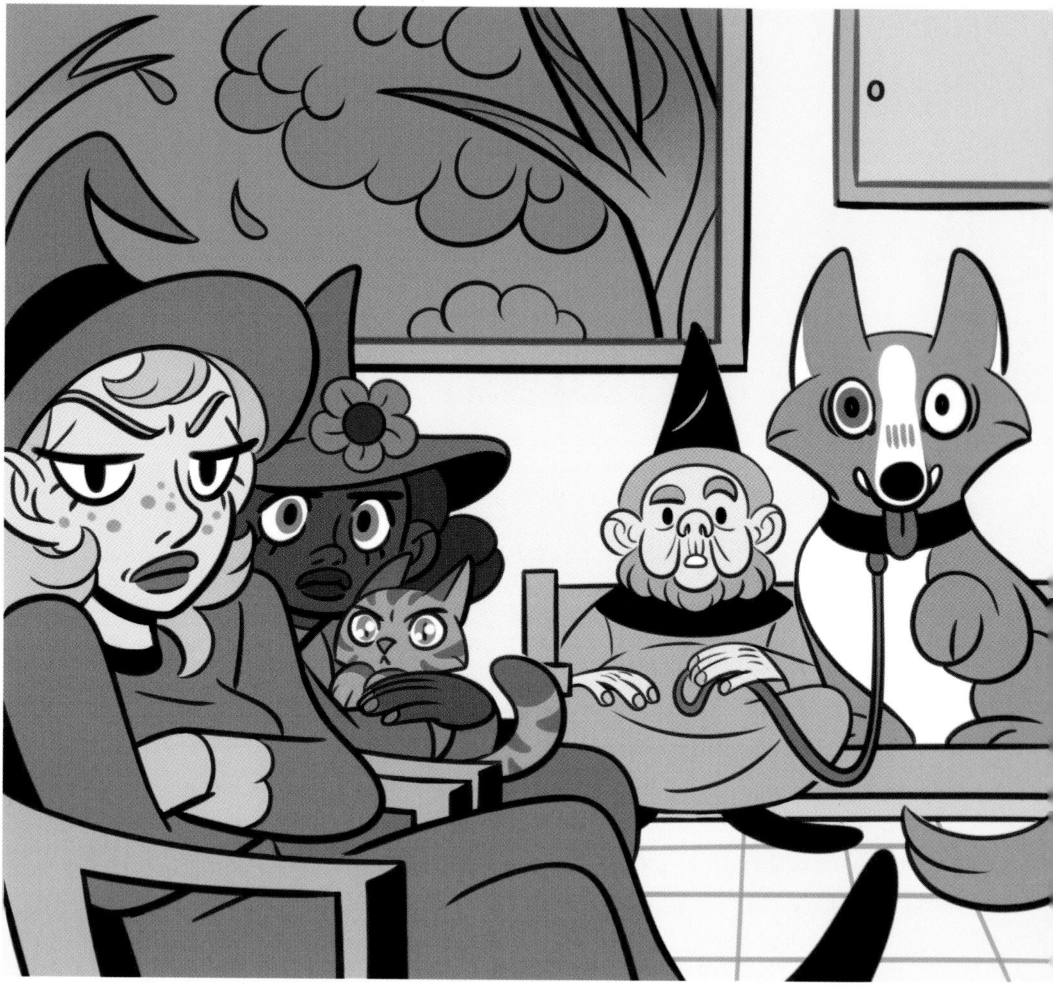

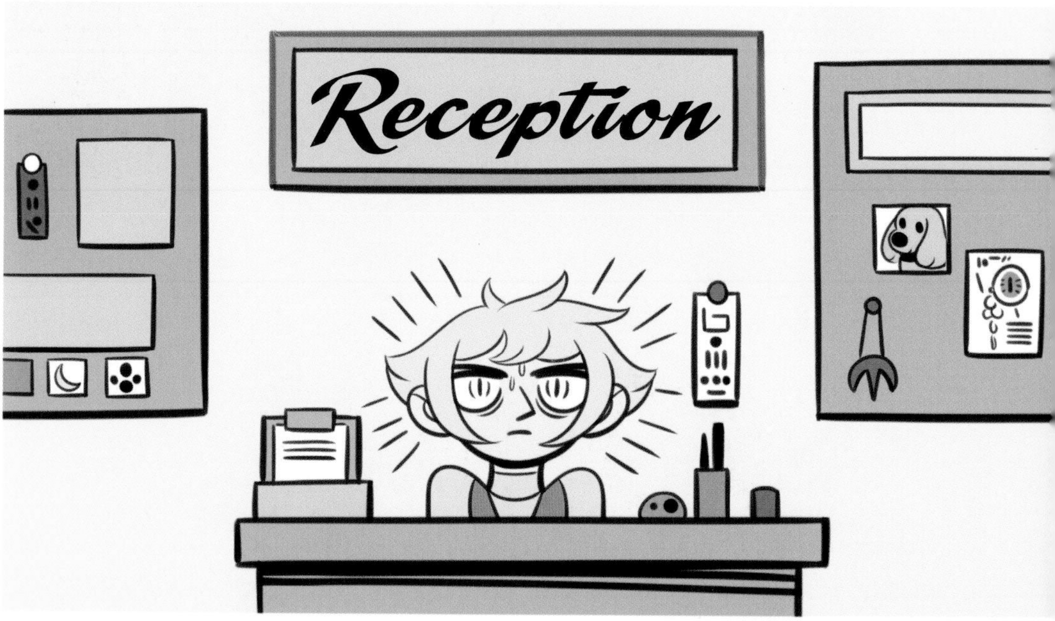
Reception

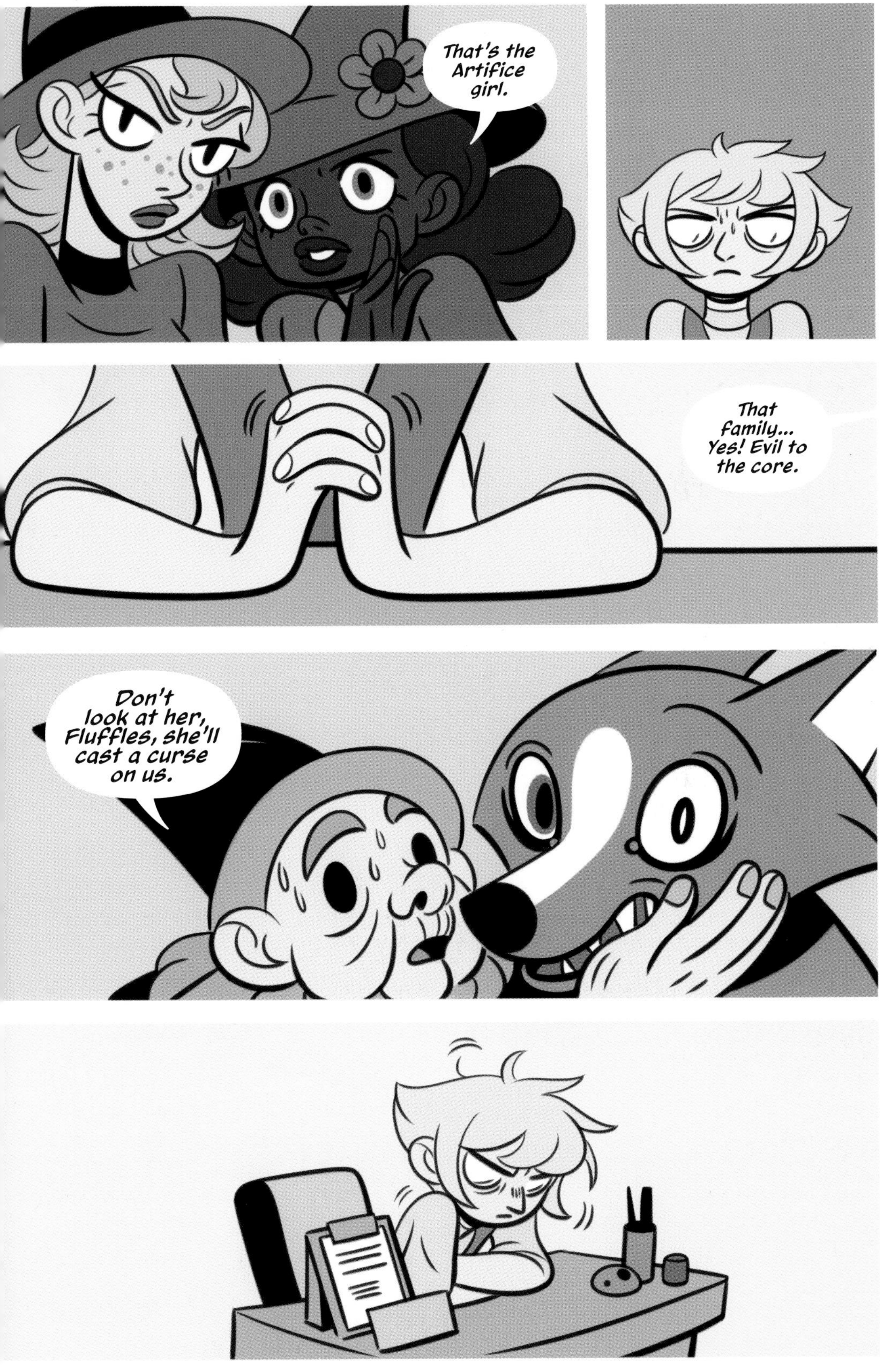
That's the Artifice girl.
That family... Yes! Evil to the core.
Don't look at her, Fluffles, she'll cast a curse on us.

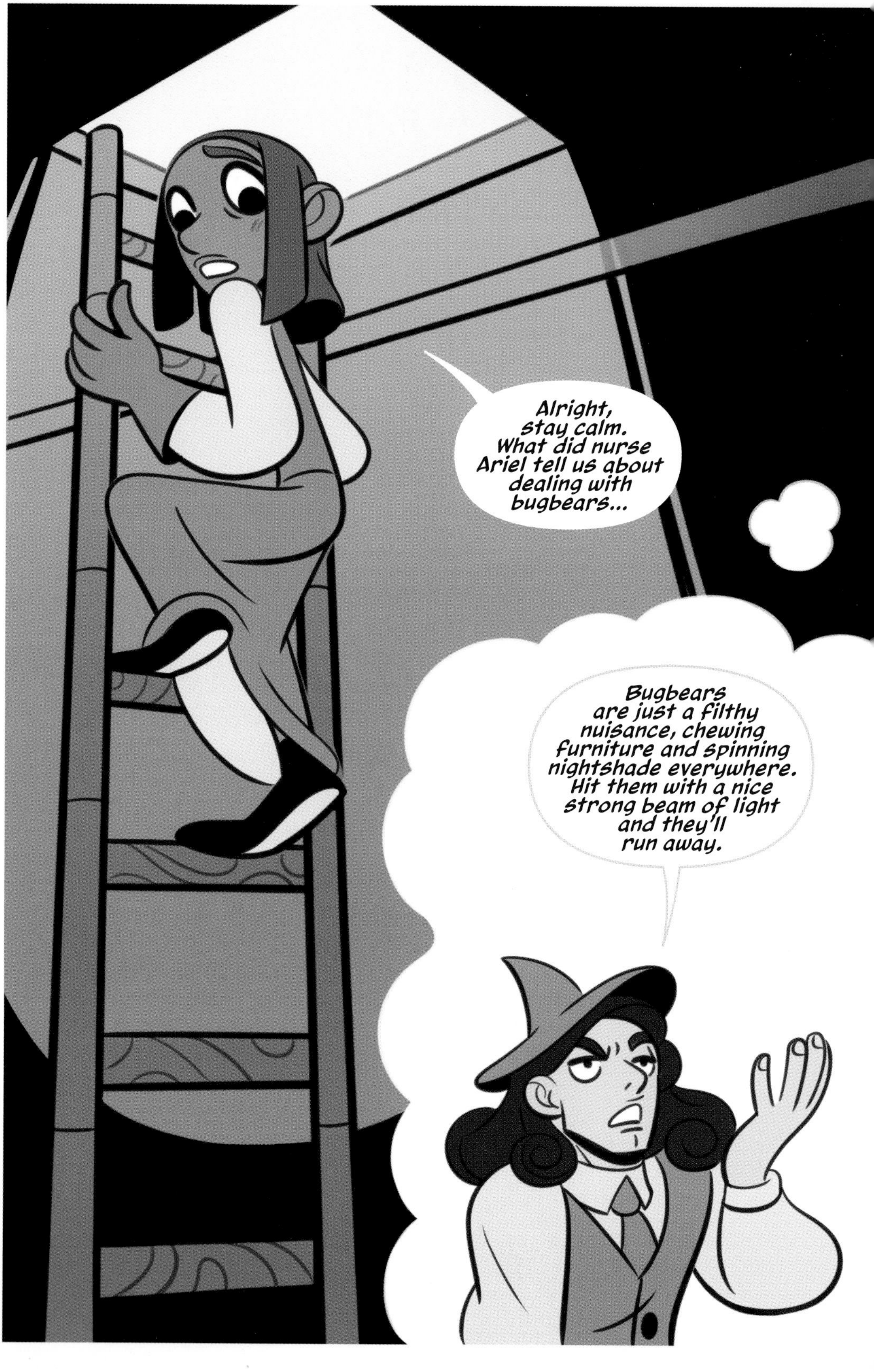
Alright, stay calm. What did nurse Ariel tell us about dealing with bugbears...
Bugbears are just a filthy nuisance, chewing furniture and spinning nightshade everywhere. Hit them with a nice strong beam of light and they'll run away.

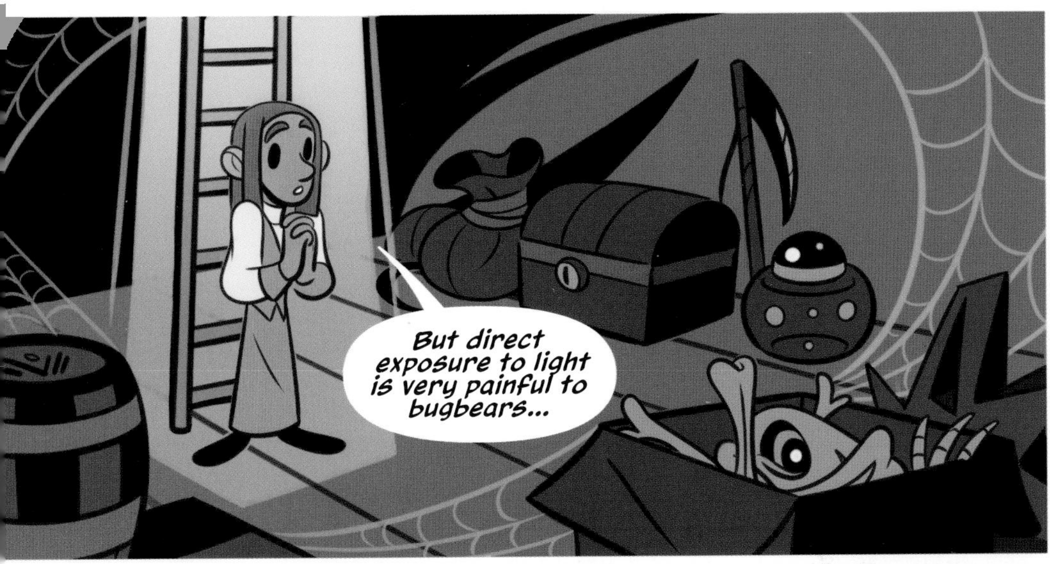
But direct exposure to light is very painful to bugbears...

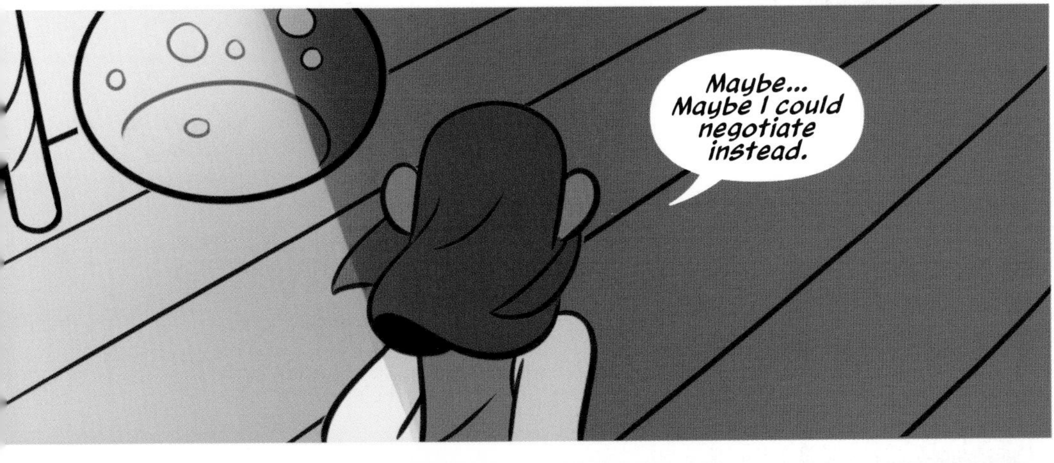
Maybe... Maybe I could negotiate instead.

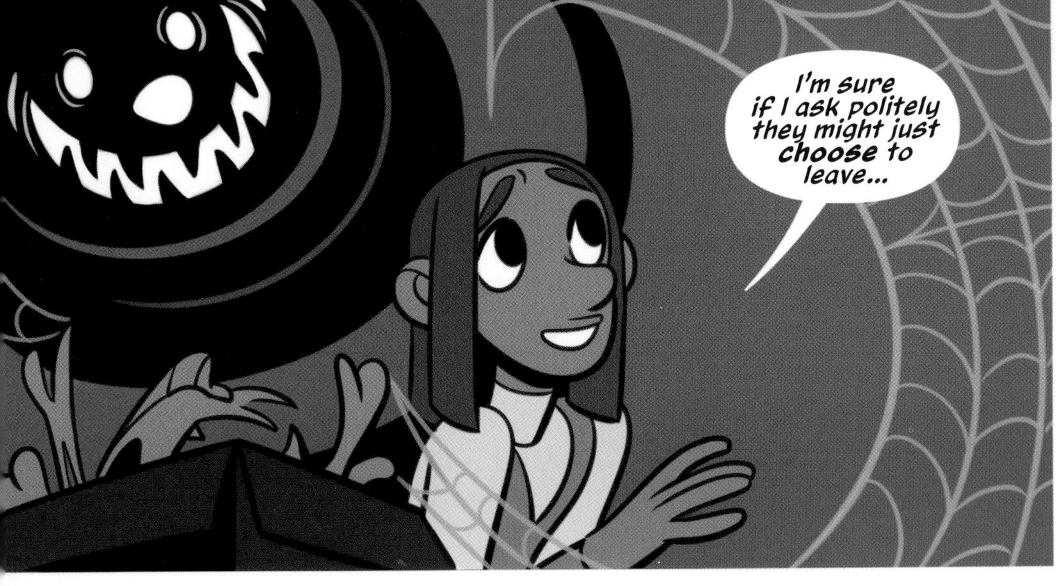
I'm sure if I ask politely they might just **choose** to leave...

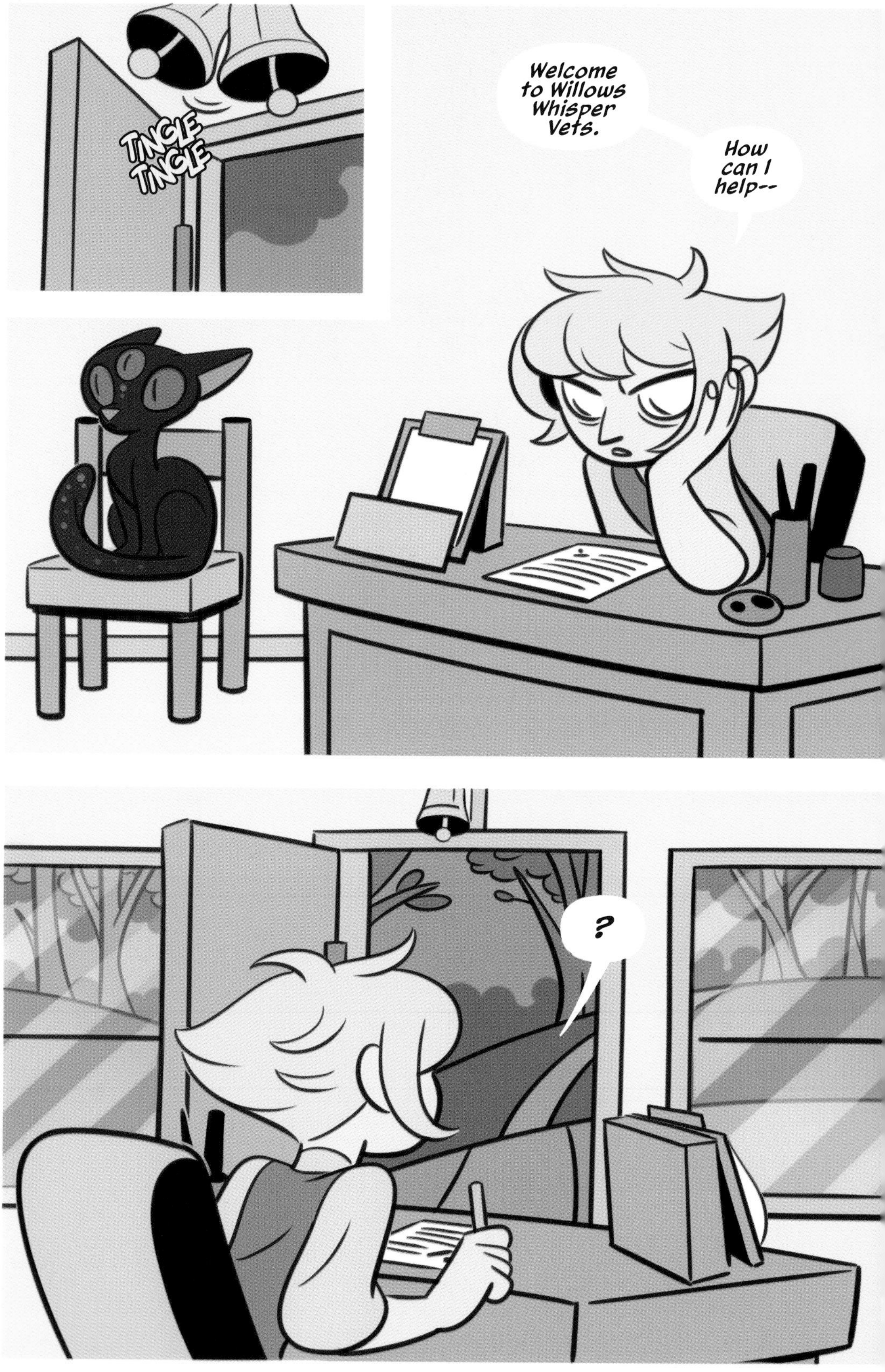
TINGLE TINGLE
Welcome to Willows Whisper Vets.
How can I help--
?

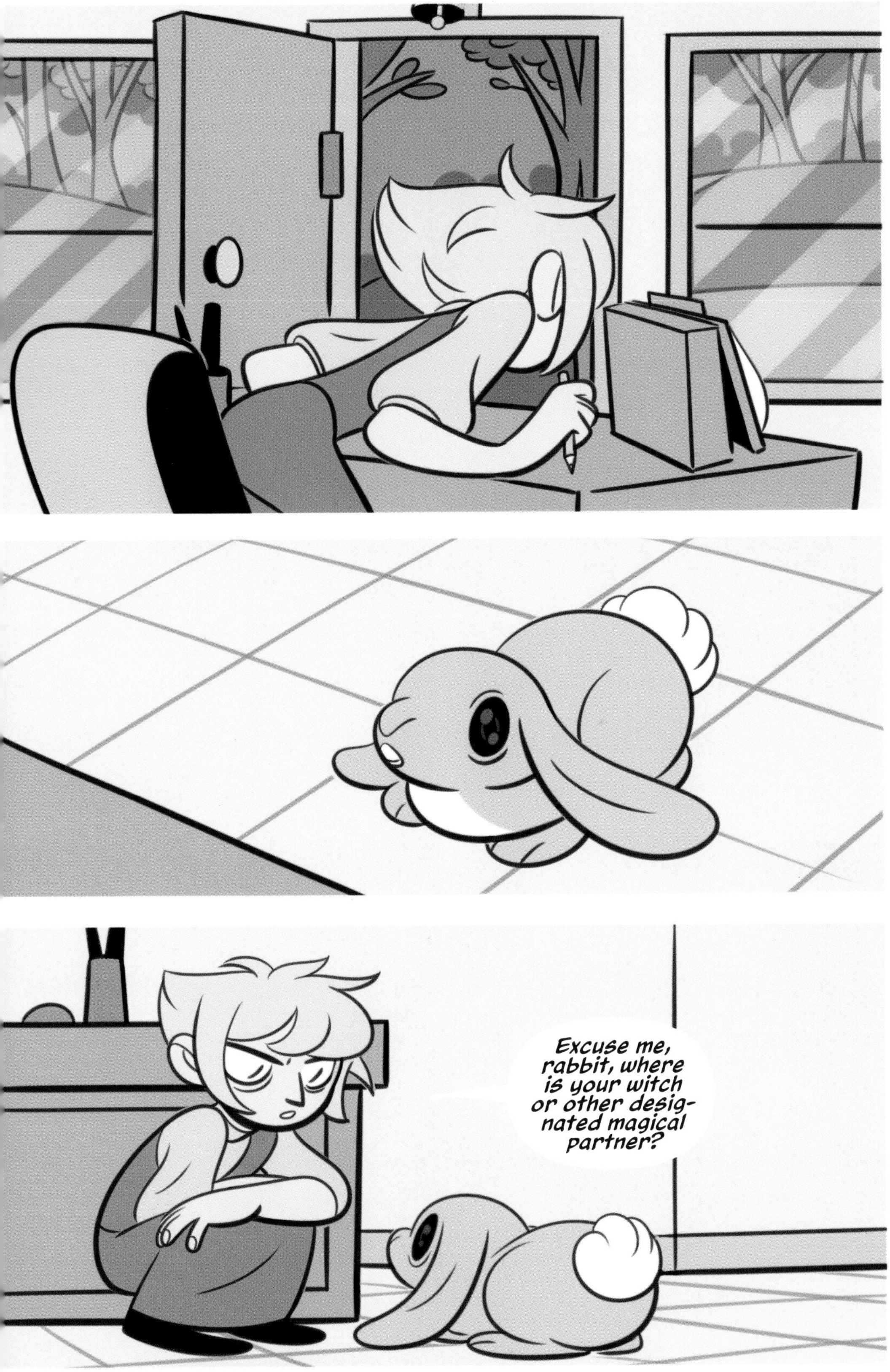
Excuse me, rabbit, where is your witch or other desig-nated magical partner?

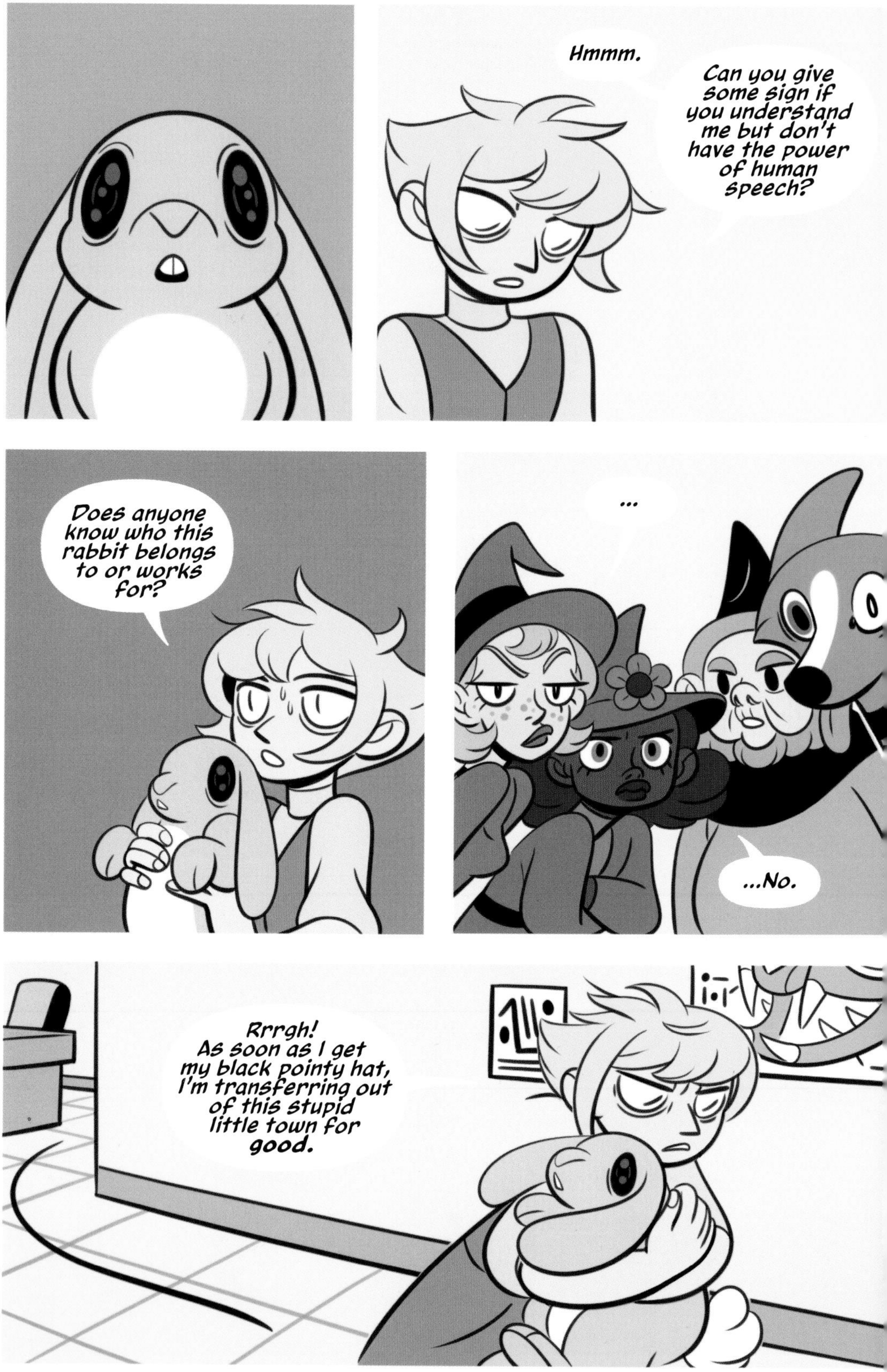
Hmmm.
Can you give some sign if you understand me but don't have the power of human speech?
Does anyone know who this rabbit belongs to or works for?
...
...No.
Rrrgh! As soon as I get my black pointy hat, I'm transferring out of this stupid little town for good.

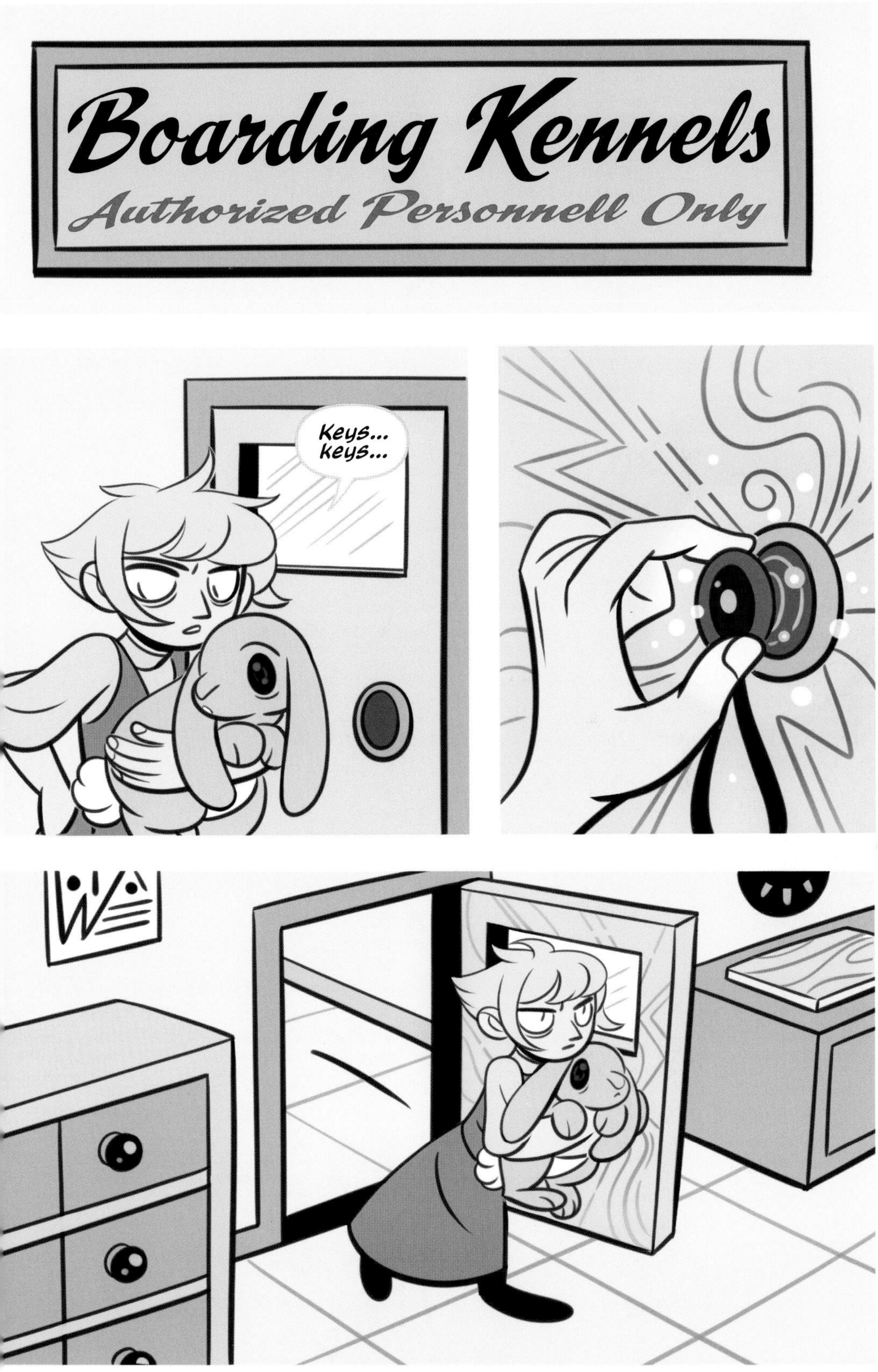
Boarding Kennels
Authorized Personnell Only
Keys... keys...

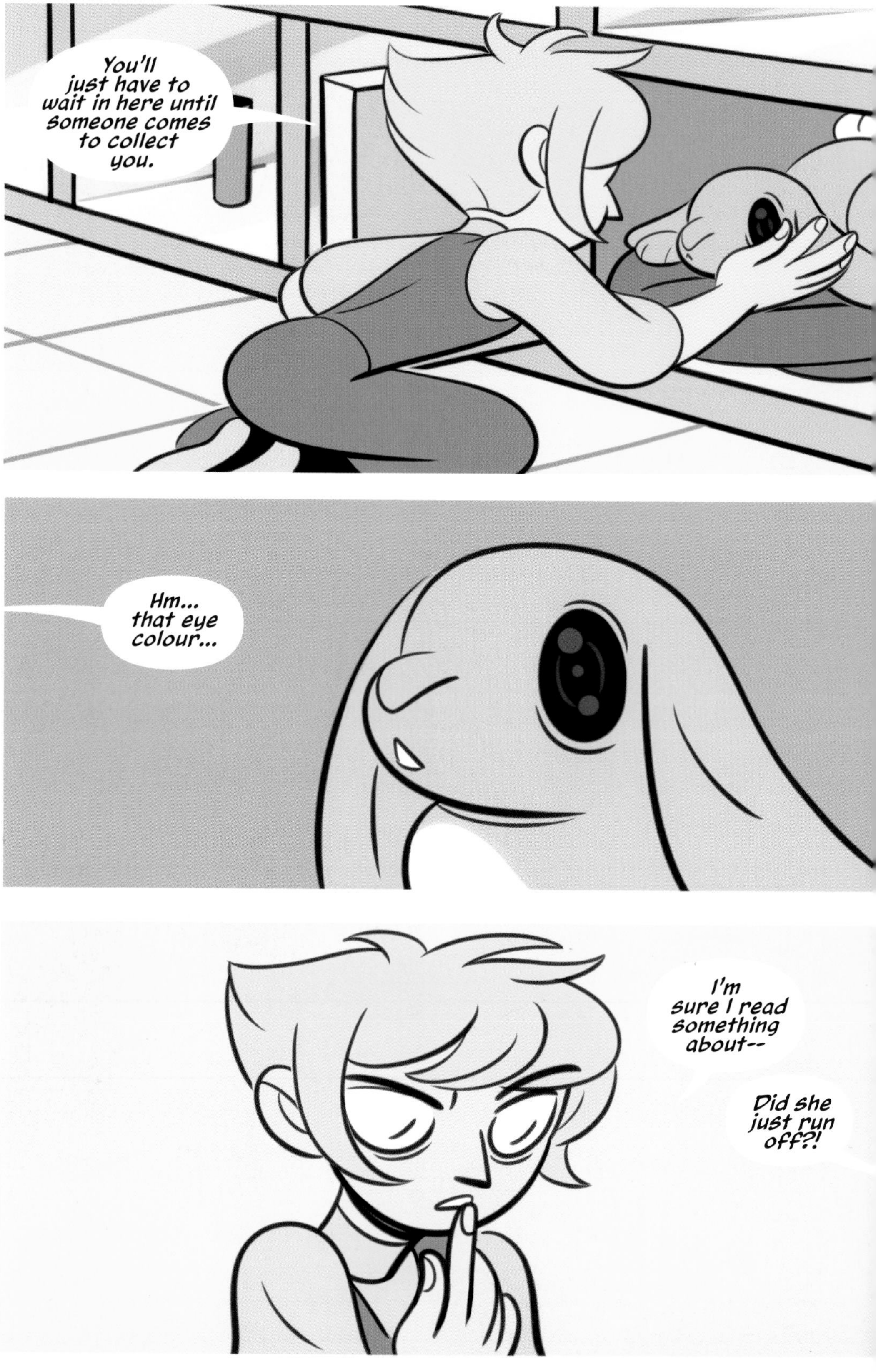
You'll just have to wait in here until someone comes to collect you.
Hm... that eye colour...
I'm sure I read something about--
Did she just run off?!

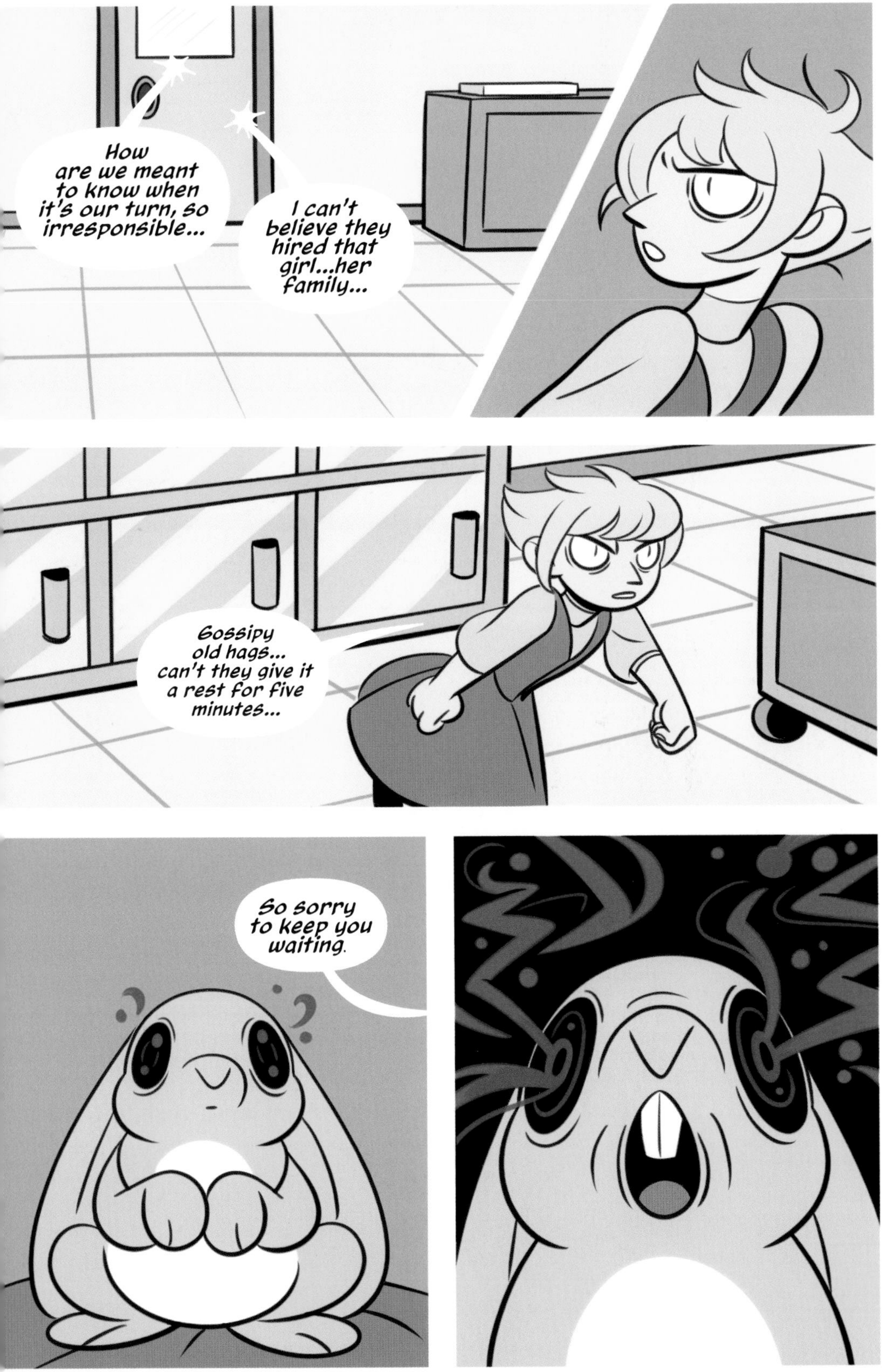
How are we meant to know when it's our turn, so irresponsible...
I can't believe they hired that girl...her family...
Gossipy old hags... can't they give it a rest for five minutes...
So sorry to keep you waiting.

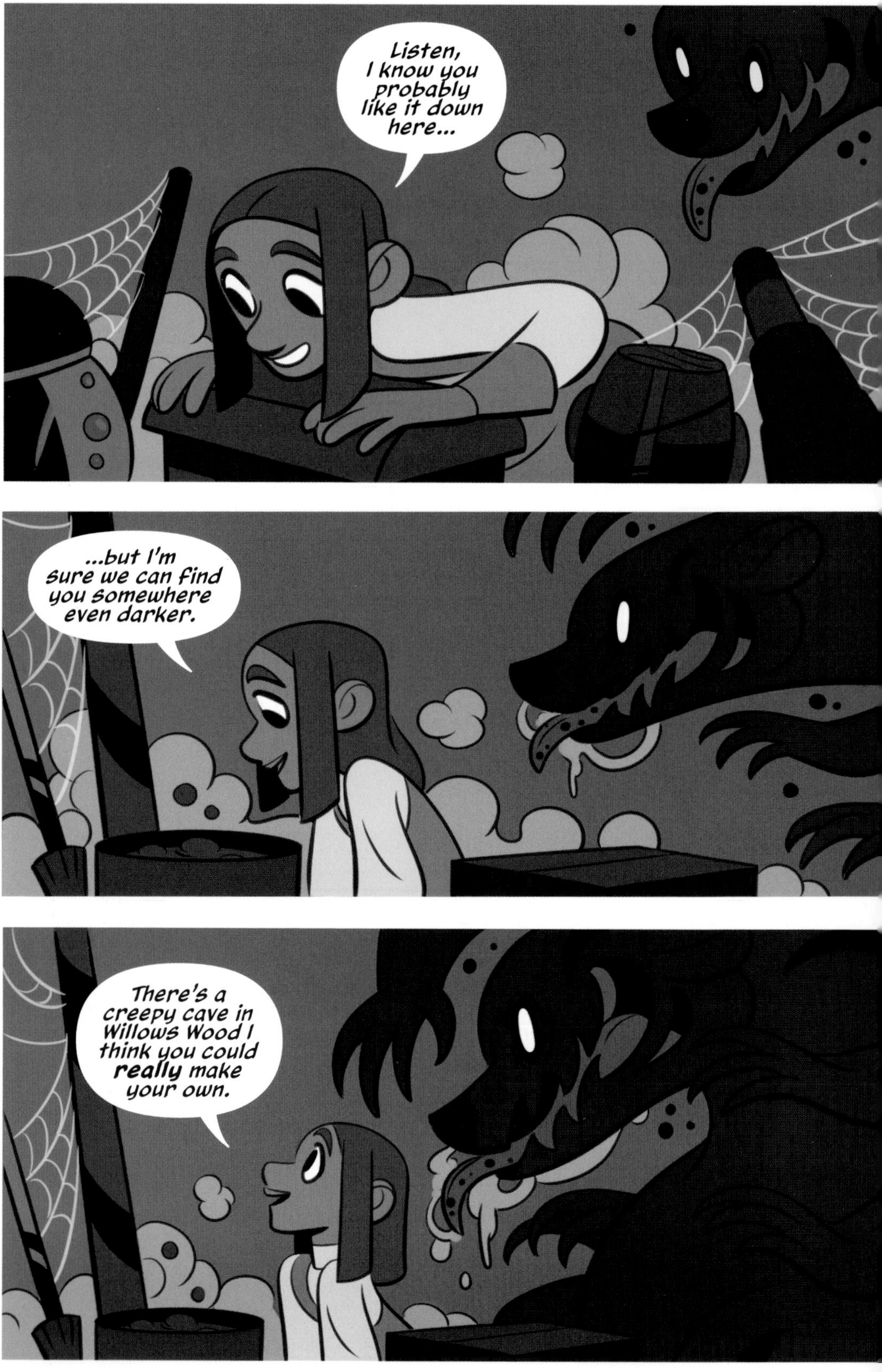
Listen, I know you probably like it down here...
...but I'm sure we can find you somewhere even darker.
There's a creepy cave in Willows Wood I think you could **really** make your own.

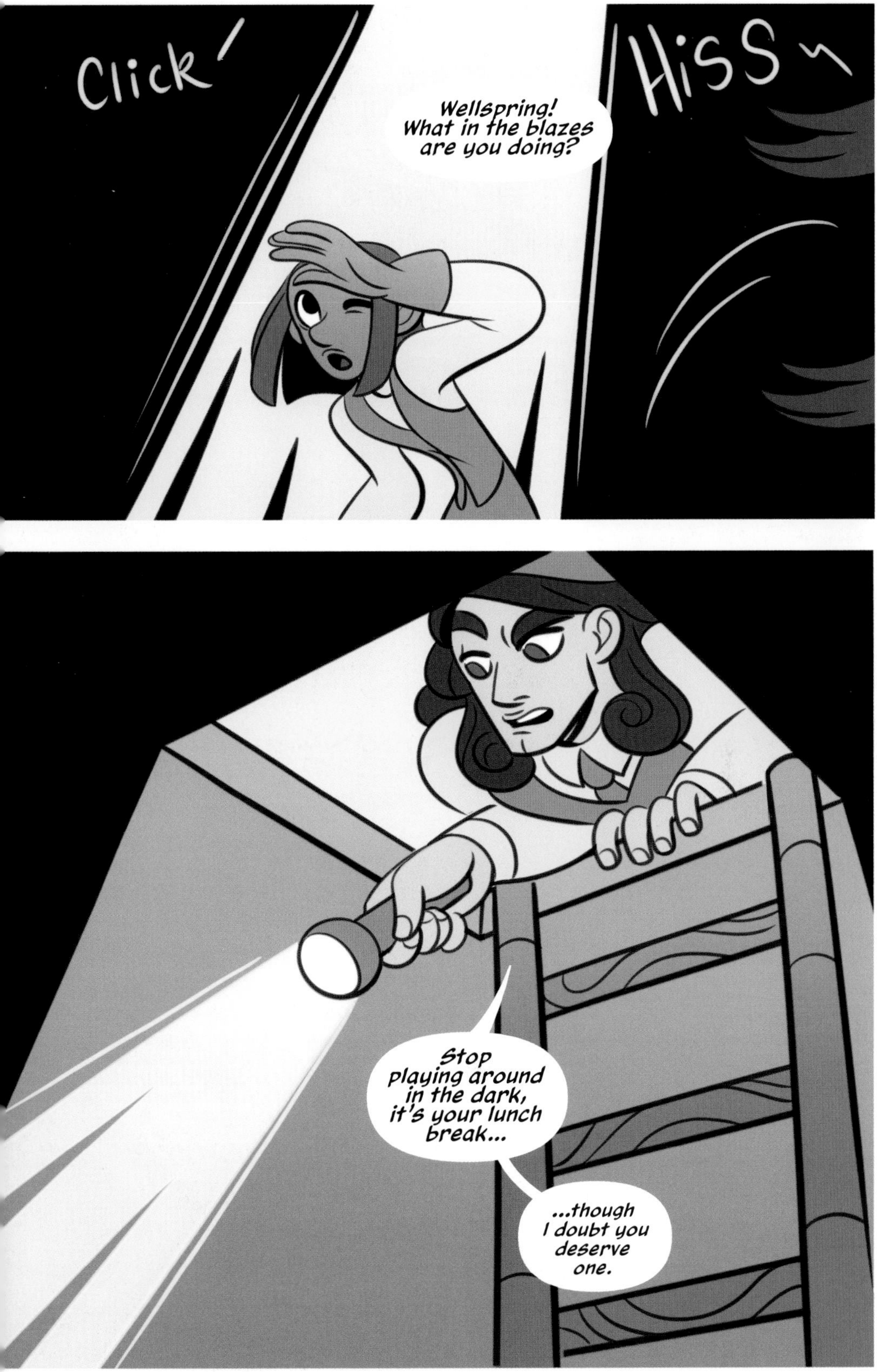
Click'
Hiss
Wellspring! What in the blazes are you doing?
Stop playing around in the dark, it's your lunch break...
...though I doubt you deserve one.

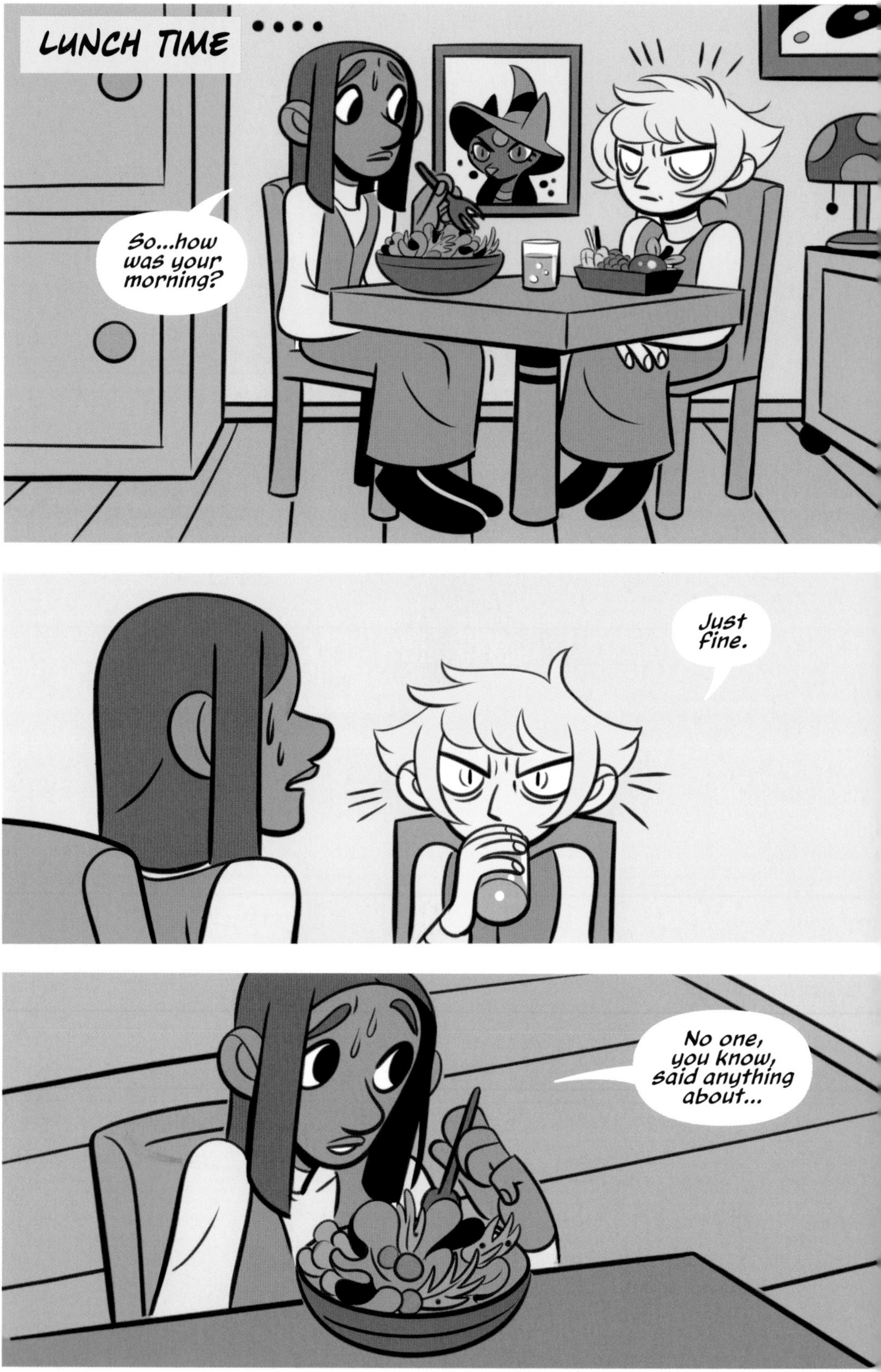
LUNCH TIME
So...how was your morning?
Just fine.
No one, you know, said anything about...

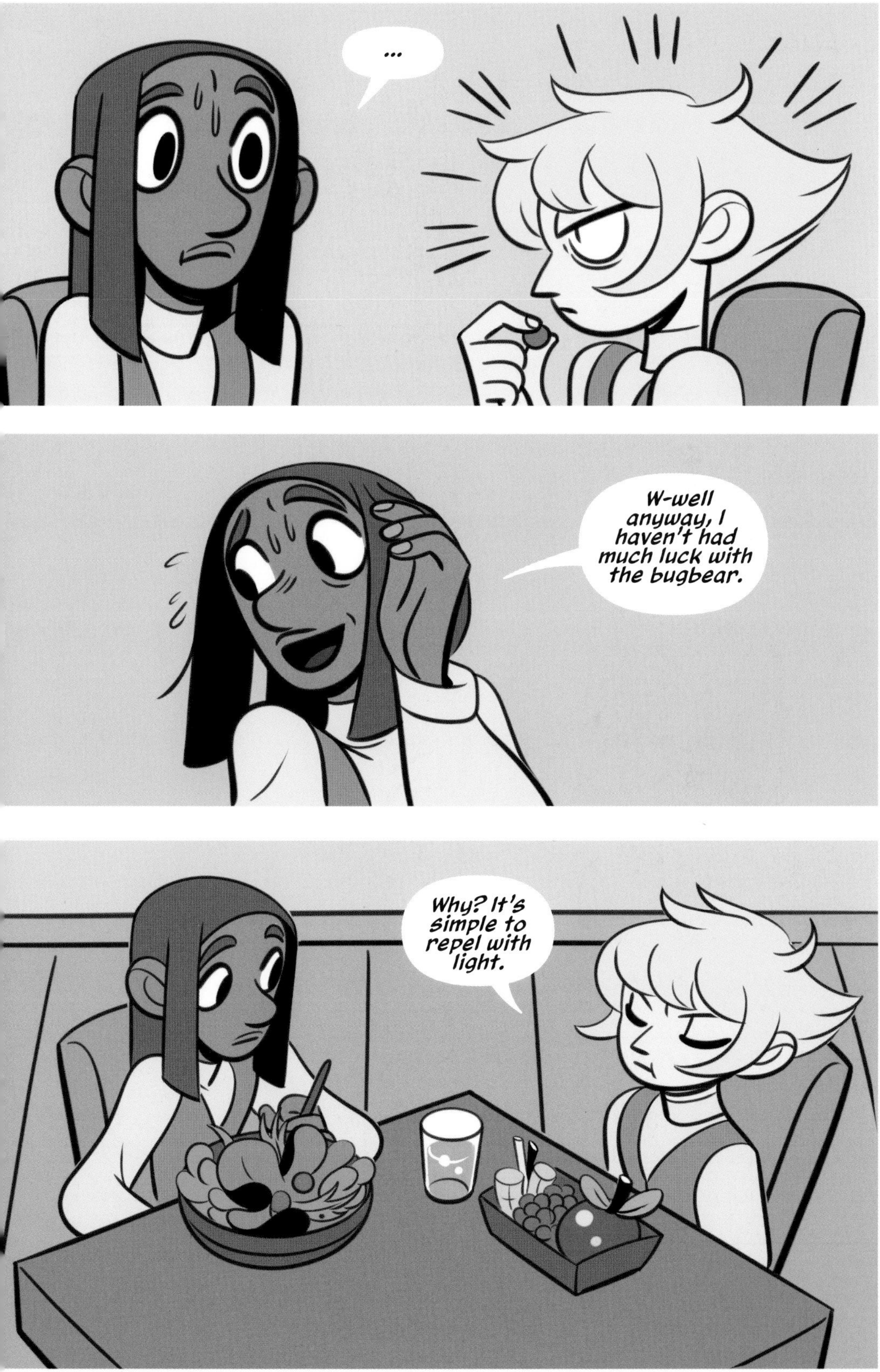
...
W-well anyway, I haven't had much luck with the bugbear.
Why? It's simple to repel with light.

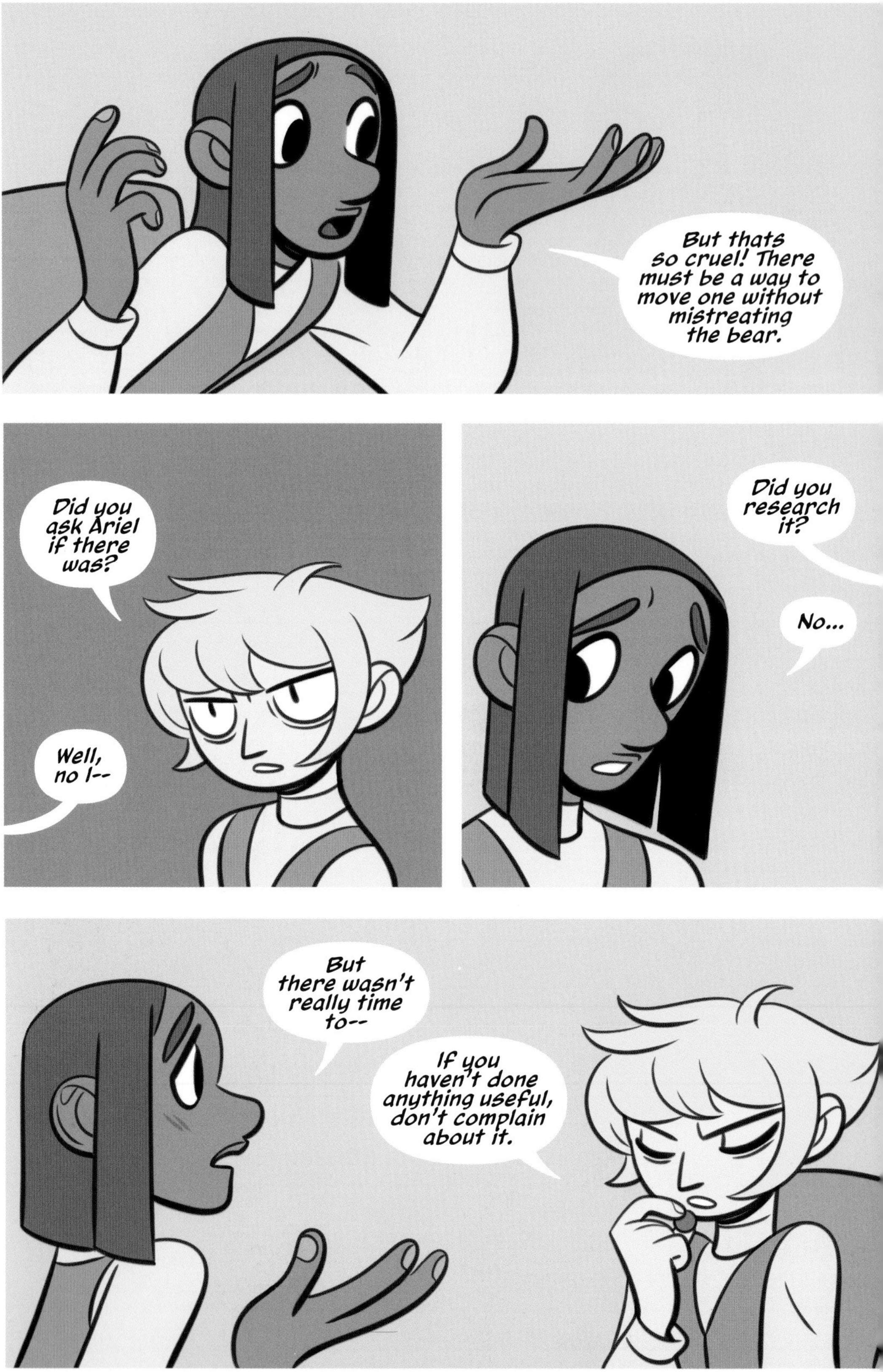
But thats so cruel! There must be a way to move one without mistreating the bear.
Did you ask Ariel if there was?
Well, no I--
Did you research it?
No...
But there wasn't really time to--
If you haven't done anything useful, don't complain about it.

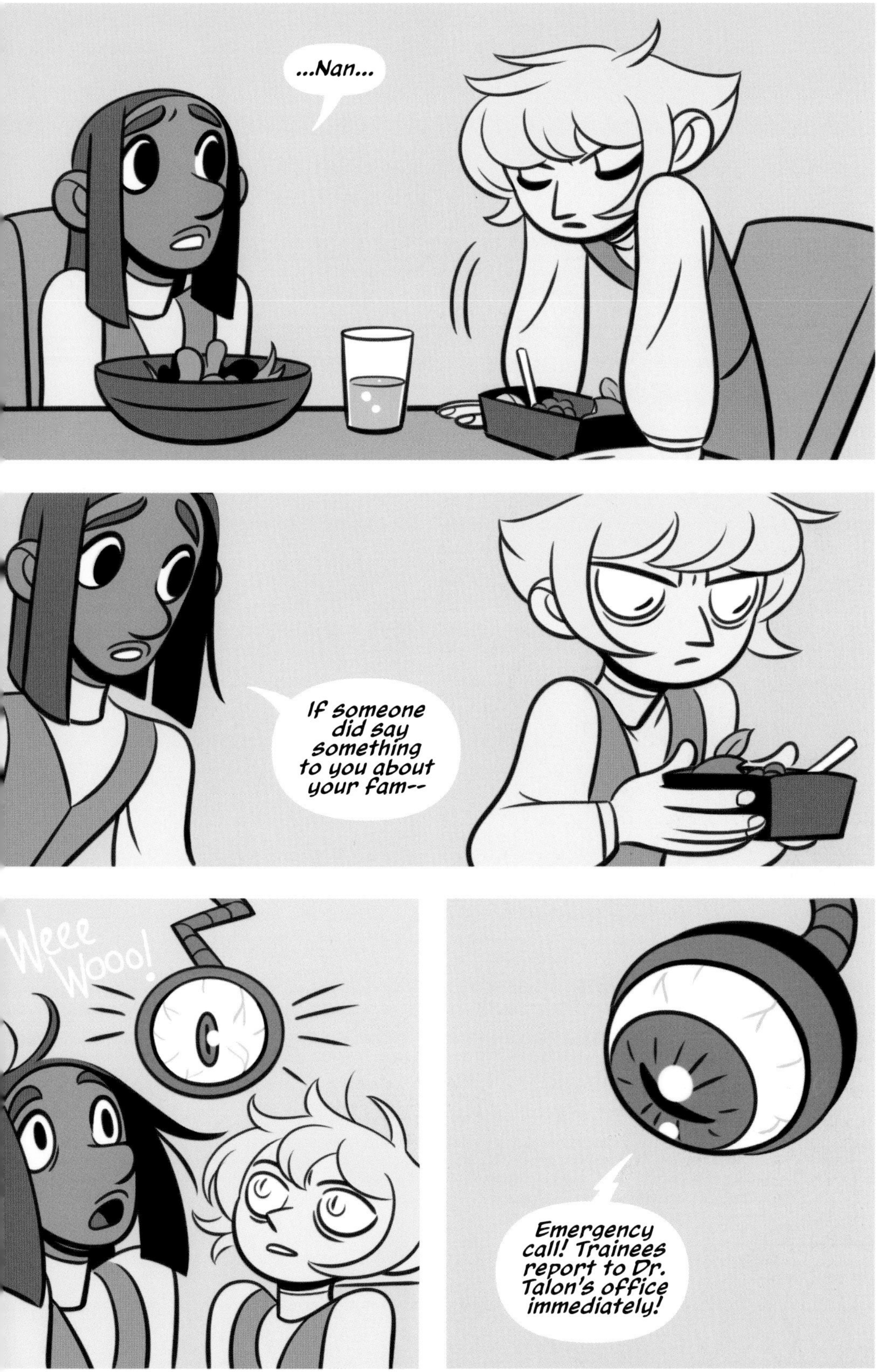
...Nan...
If someone did say something to you about your fam--
Weee Wooo!
Emergency call! Trainees report to Dr. Talon's office immediately!

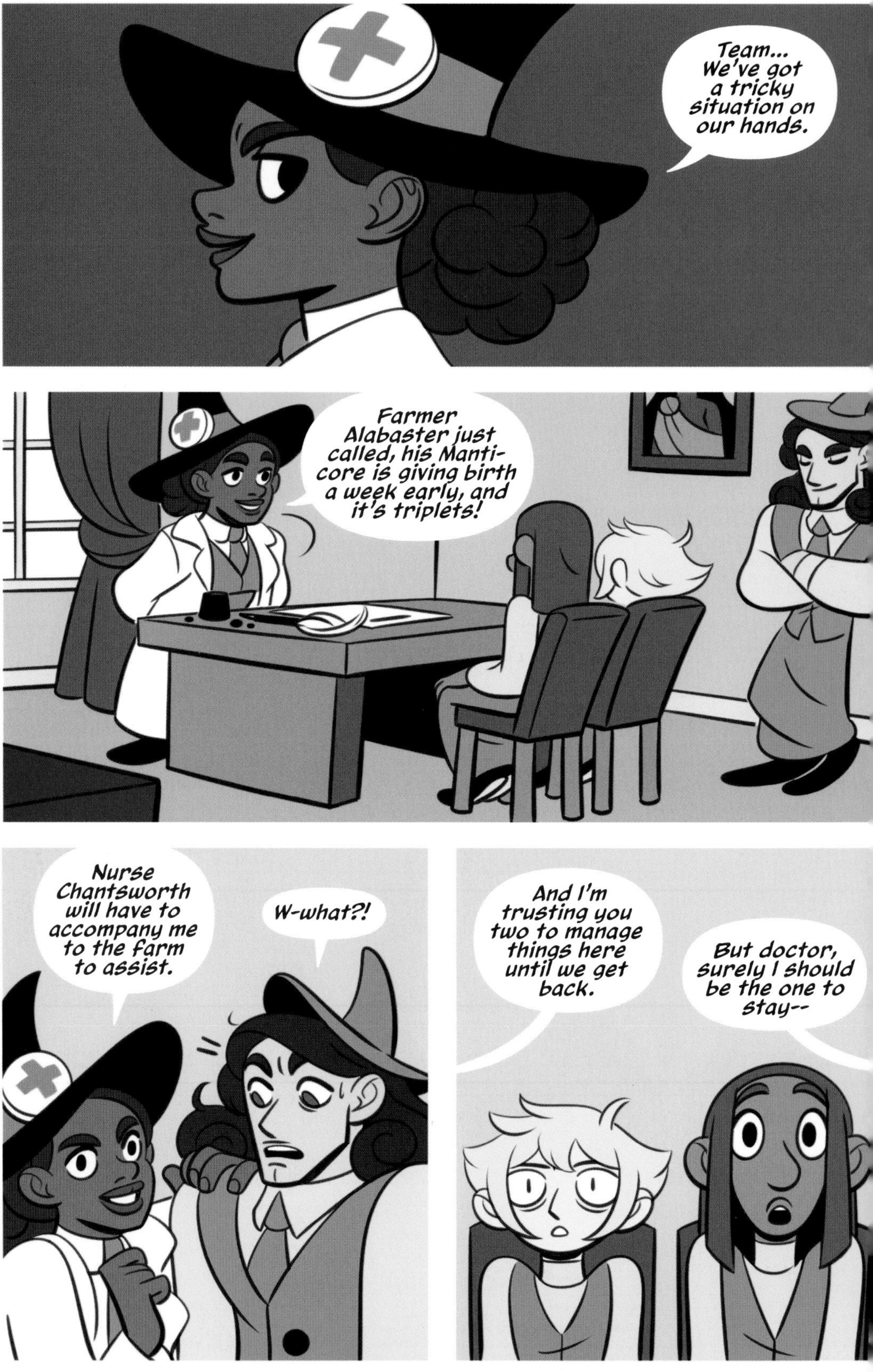
Team... We've got a tricky situation on our hands.
Farmer Alabaster just called, his Manti-core is giving birth a week early, and it's triplets!
Nurse Chantsworth will have to accompany me to the farm to assist.
W-what?!
And I'm trusting you two to manage things here until we get back.
But doctor, surely I should be the one to stay--

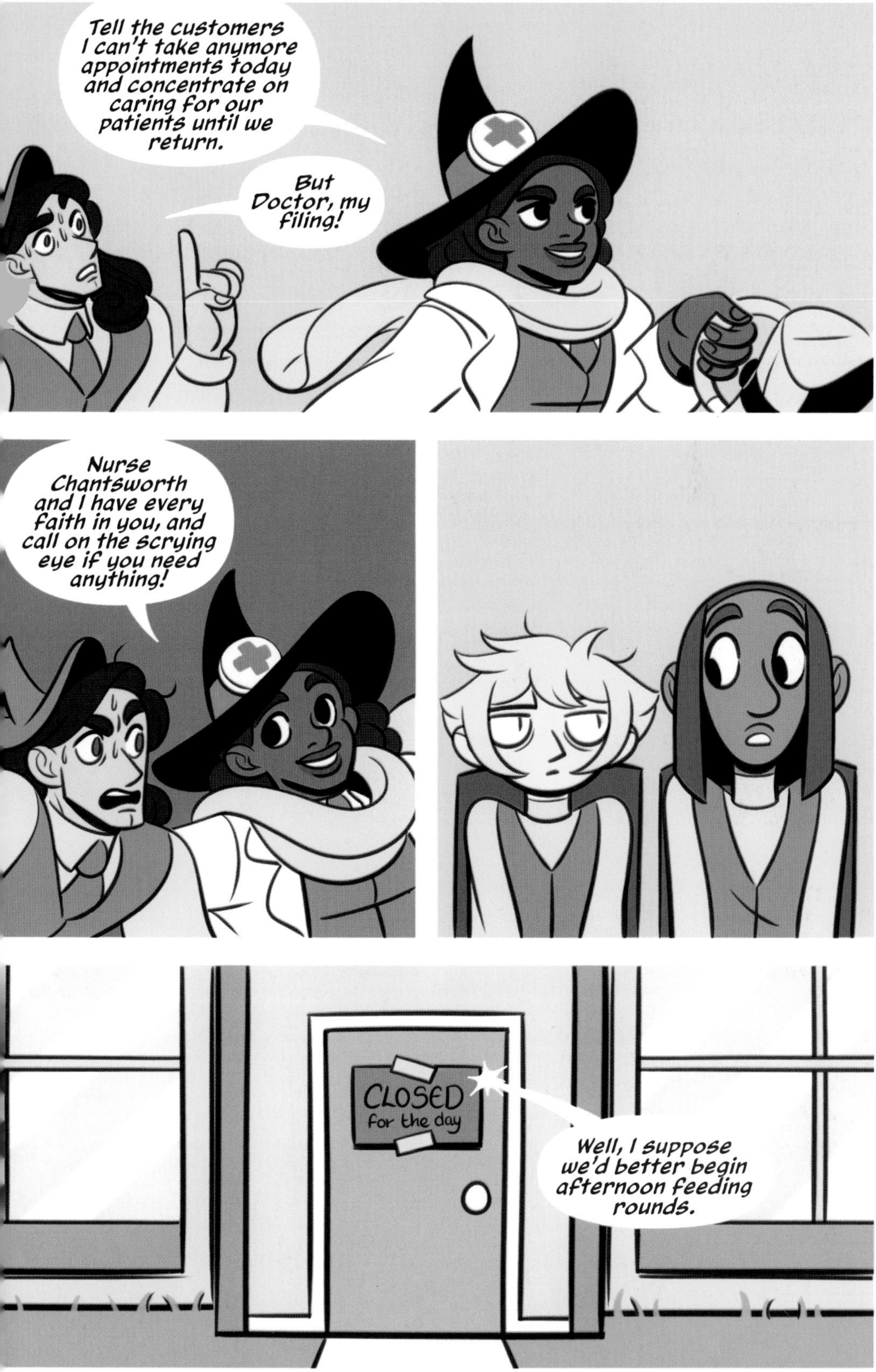
Tell the customers I can't take anymore appointments today and concentrate on caring for our patients until we return.
But Doctor, my filing!
Nurse Chantsworth and I have every faith in you, and call on the scrying eye if you need anything!
CLOSED for the day
Well, I suppose we'd better begin afternoon feeding rounds.

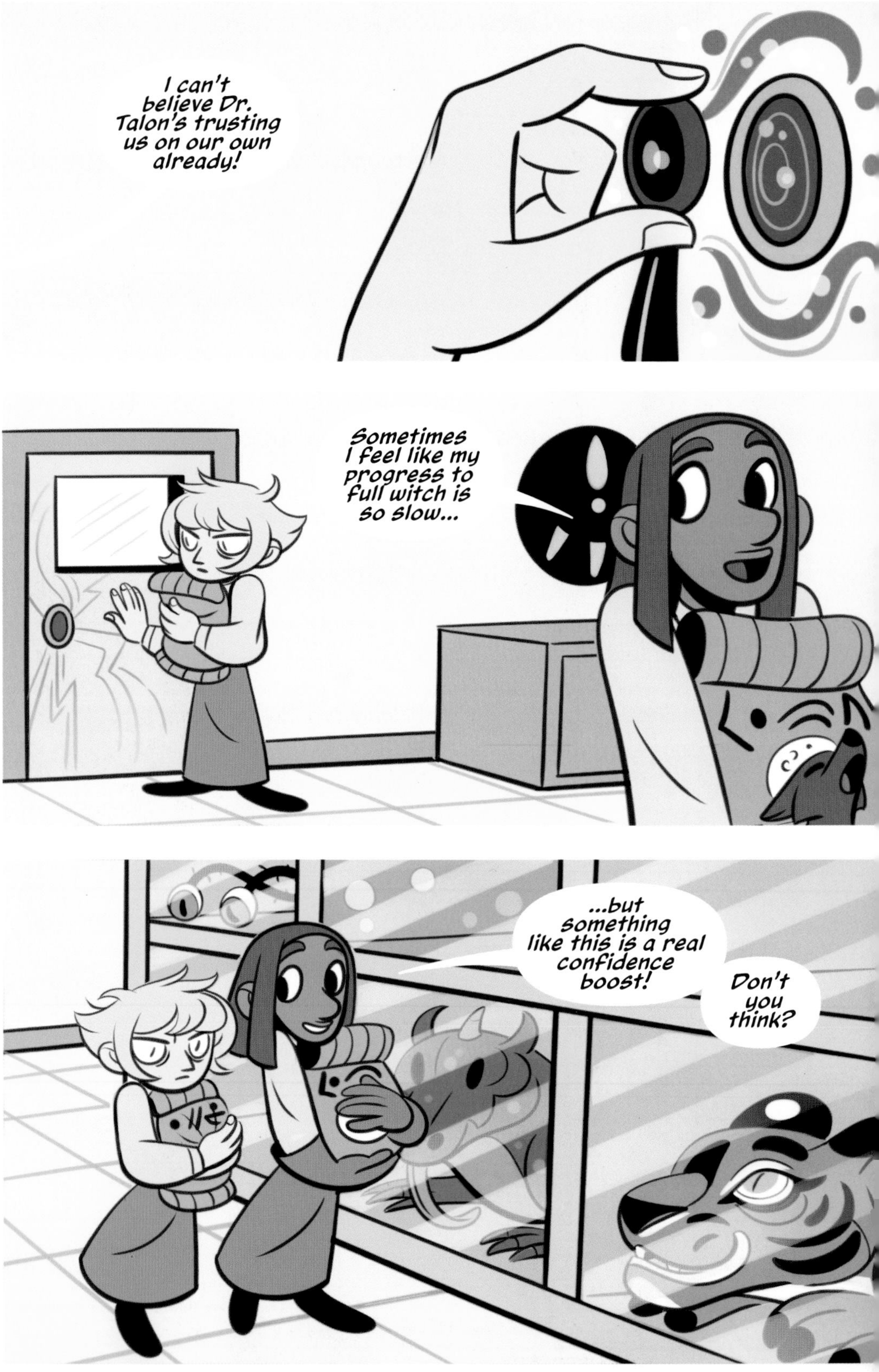
I can't believe Dr. Talon's trusting us on our own already!
Sometimes I feel like my progress to full witch is so slow...
...but something like this is a real confidence boost!
Don't you think?

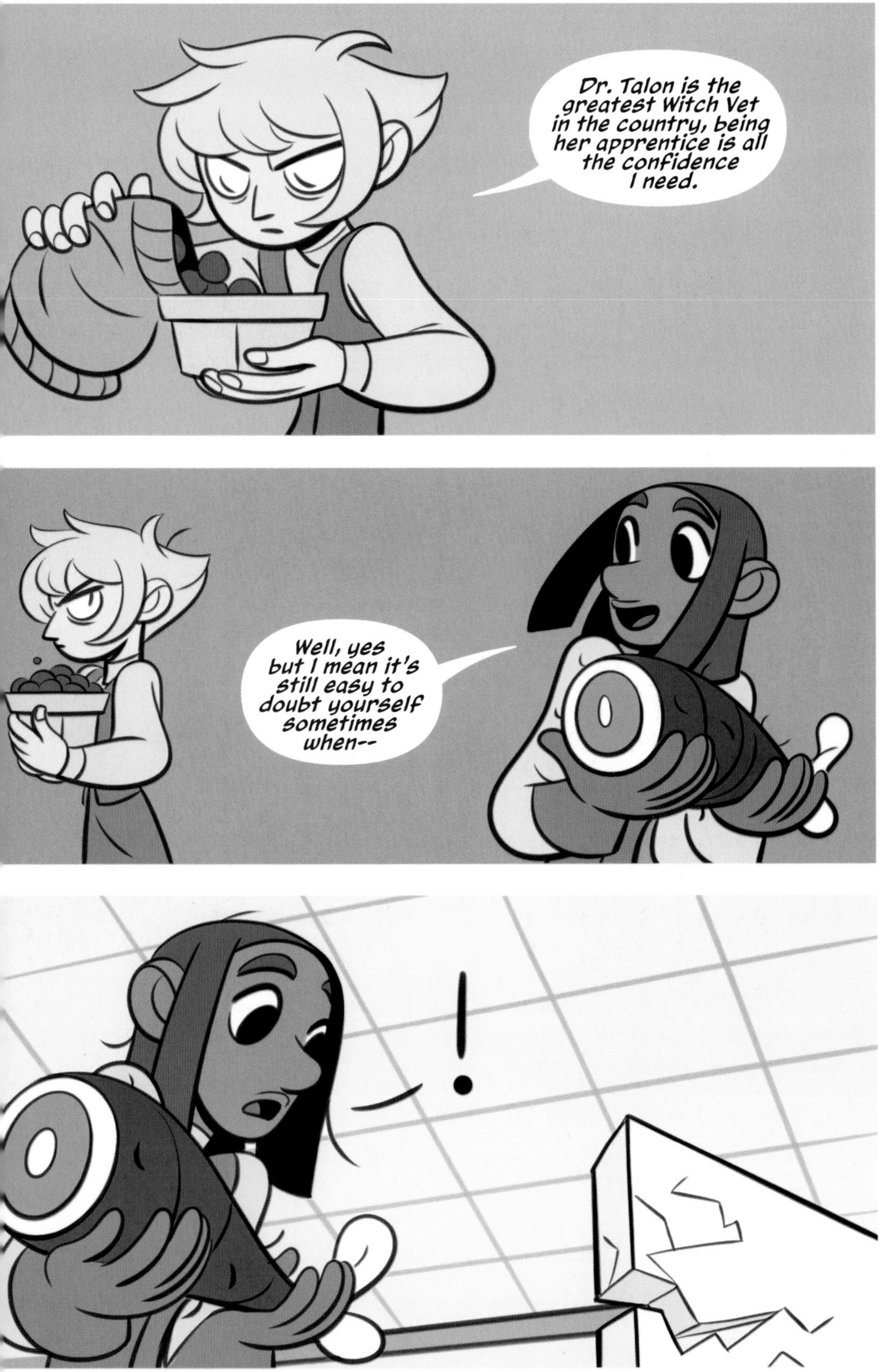
Dr. Talon is the greatest Witch Vet in the country, being her apprentice is all the confidence I need.
Well, yes but I mean it's still easy to doubt yourself sometimes when--
!

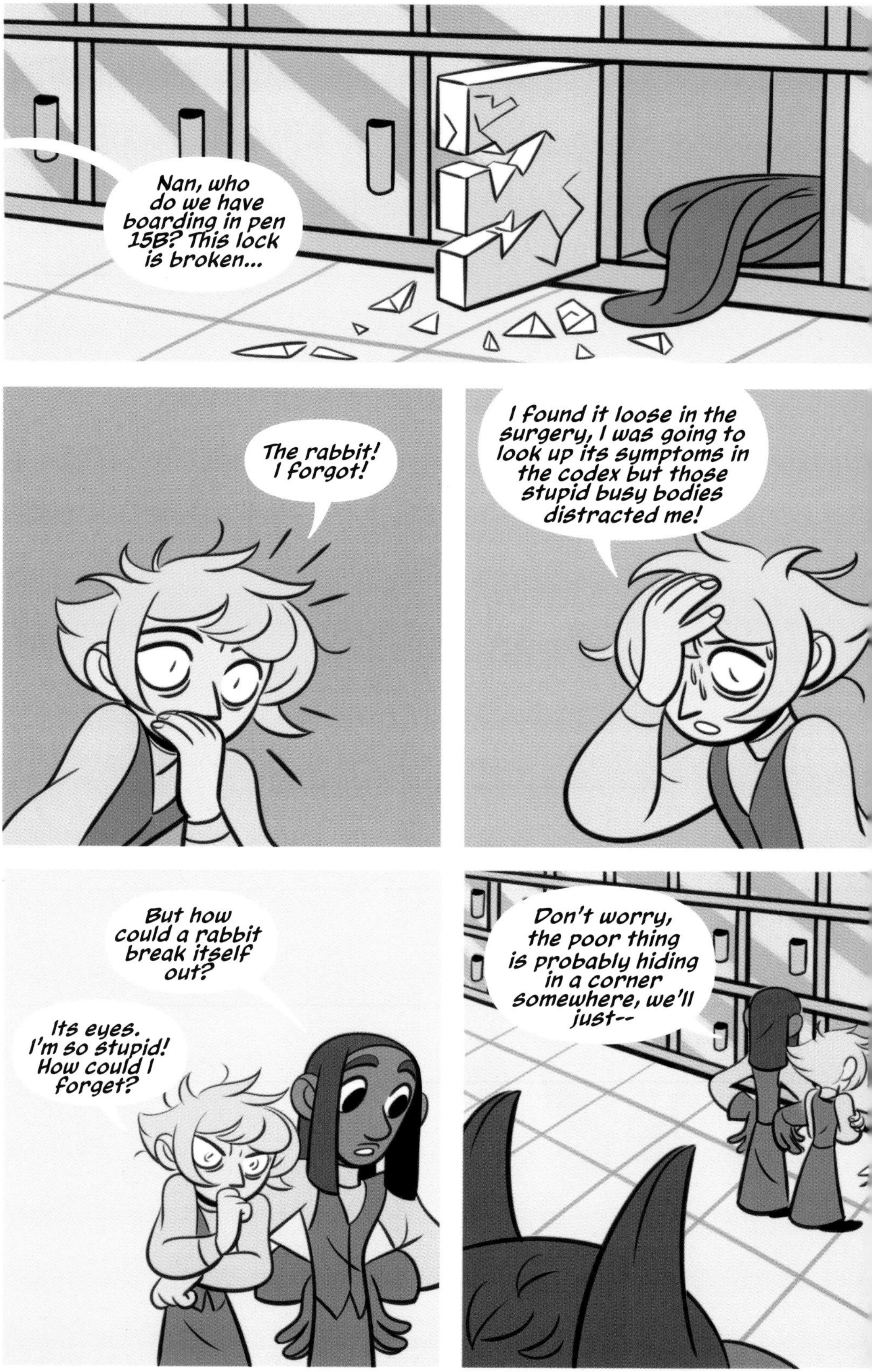
Nan, who do we have boarding in pen 15B? This lock is broken...
The rabbit! I forgot!
I found it loose in the surgery, I was going to look up its symptoms in the codex but those stupid busy bodies distracted me!
But how could a rabbit break itself out?
Its eyes. I'm so stupid! How could I forget?
Don't worry, the poor thing is probably hiding in a corner somewhere, we'll just--

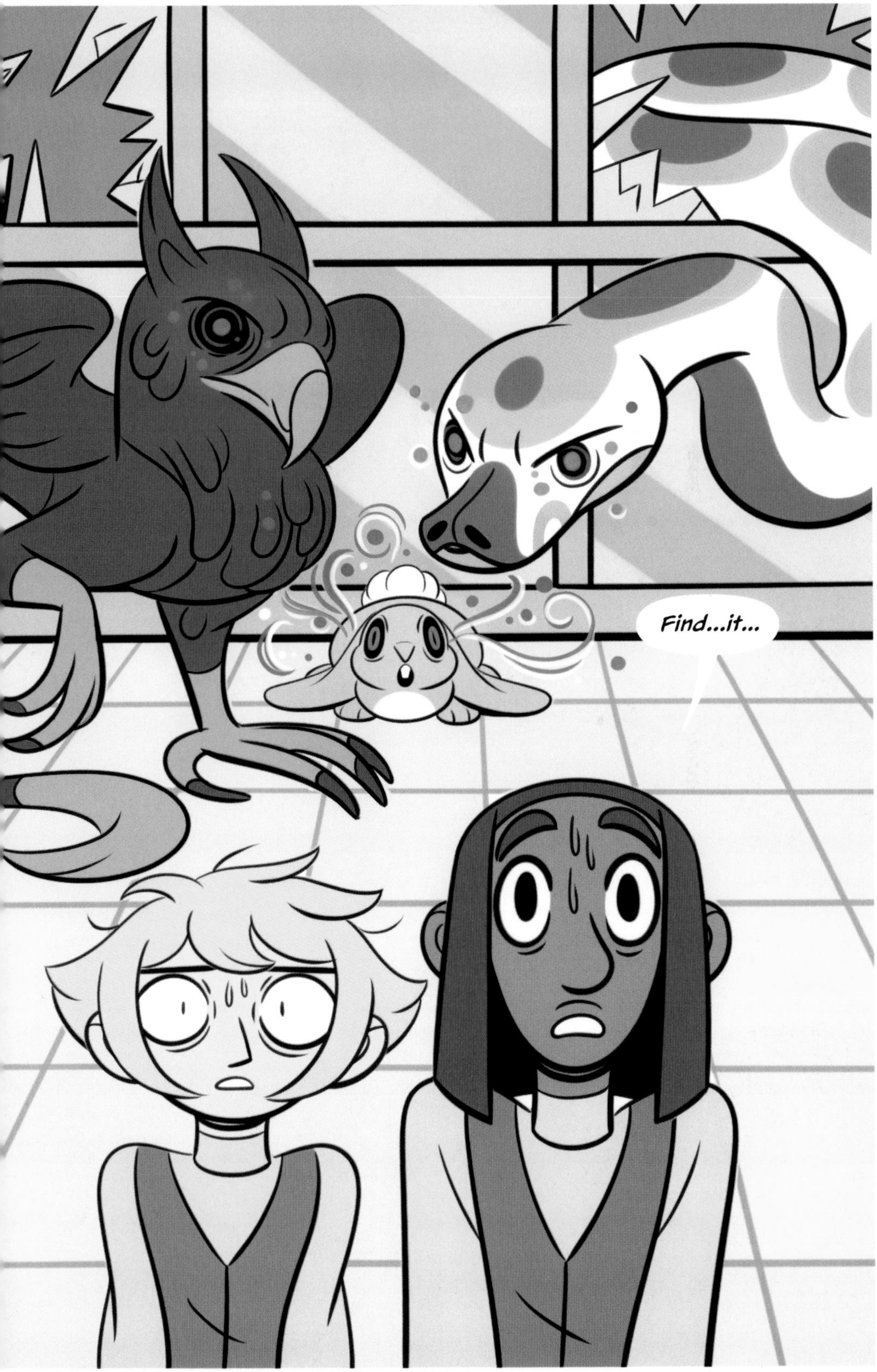
Find...it...

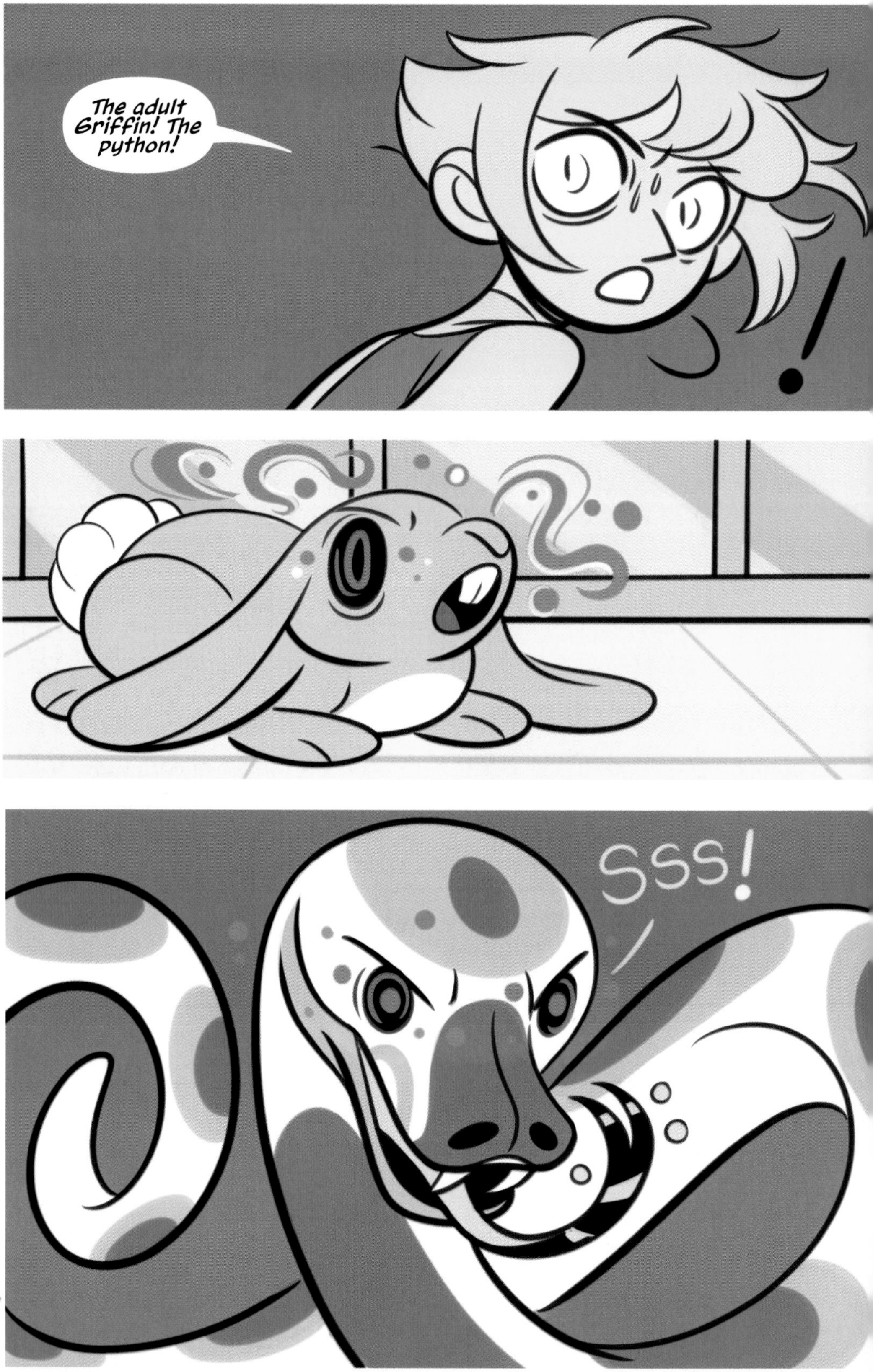

The adult Griffin! The python!
SSS!

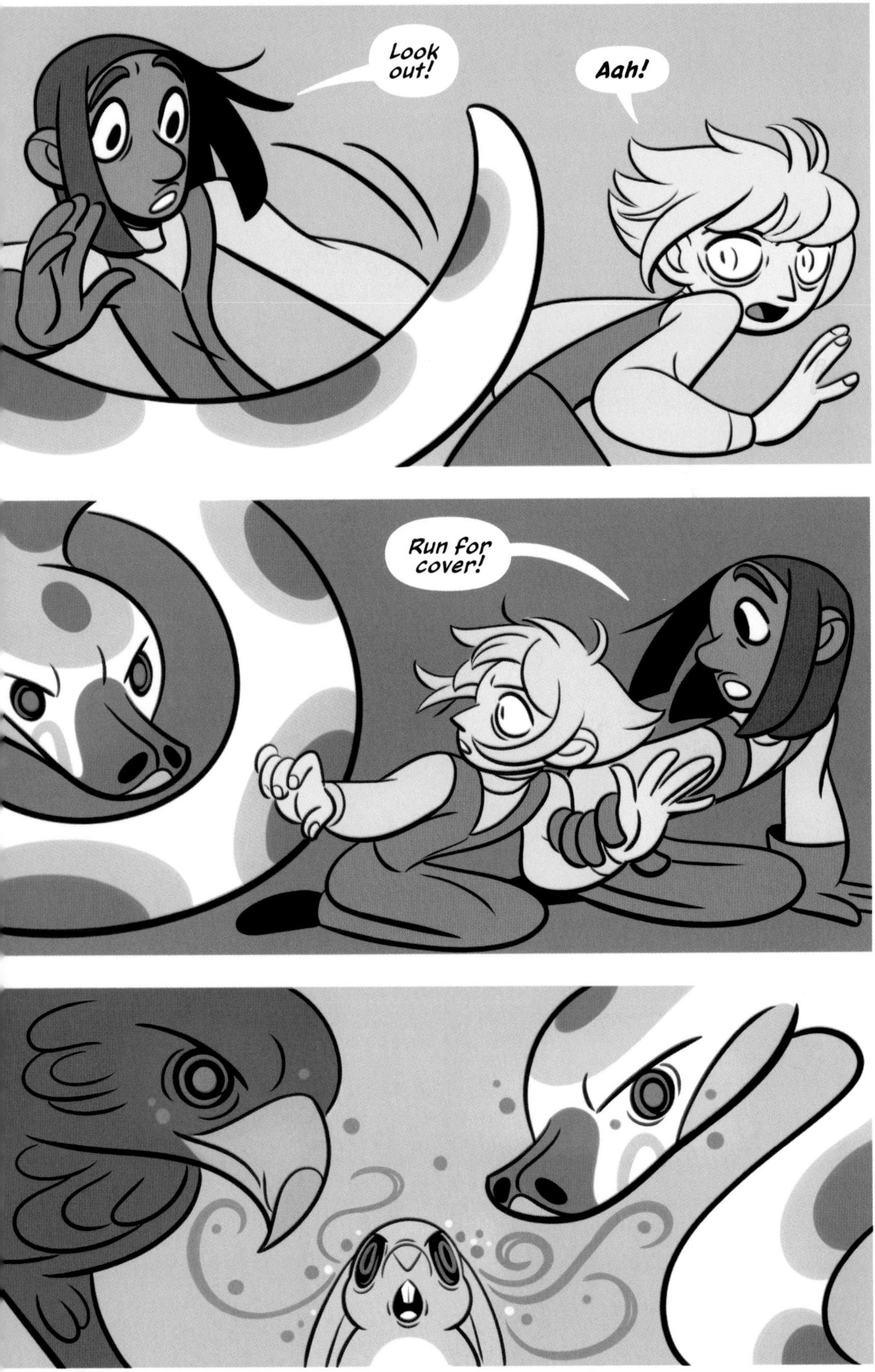
Look out!
Aah!
Run for cover!

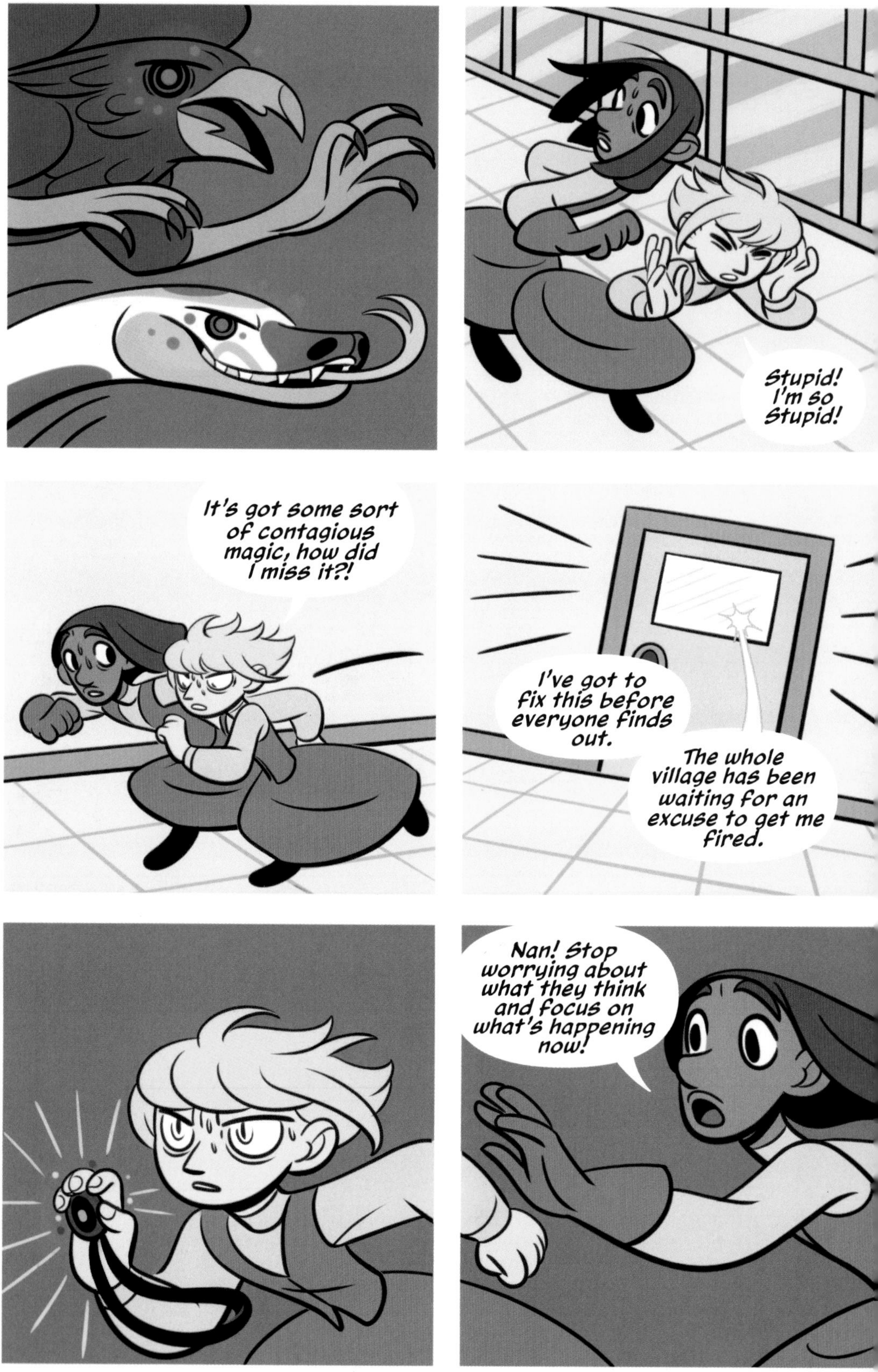
Stupid! I'm so Stupid!
It's got some sort of contagious magic, how did I miss it?!
I've got to fix this before everyone finds out.
The whole village has been waiting for an excuse to get me fired.
Nan! Stop worrying about what they think and focus on what's happening now!

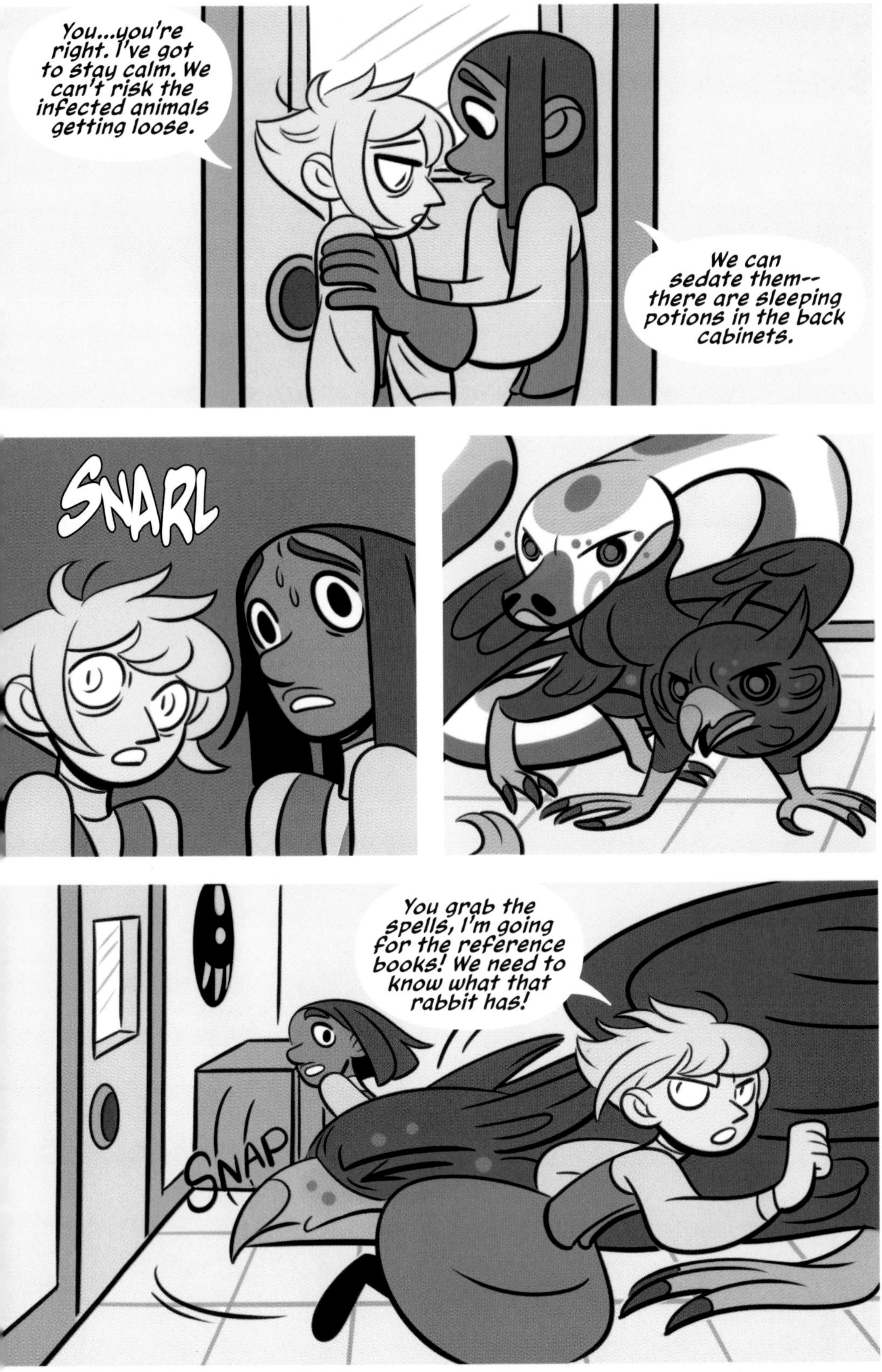
You...you're right. I've got to stay calm. We can't risk the infected animals getting loose.
We can sedate them--there are sleeping potions in the back cabinets.
SNARL
You grab the spells, I'm going for the reference books! We need to know what that rabbit has!
SNAP

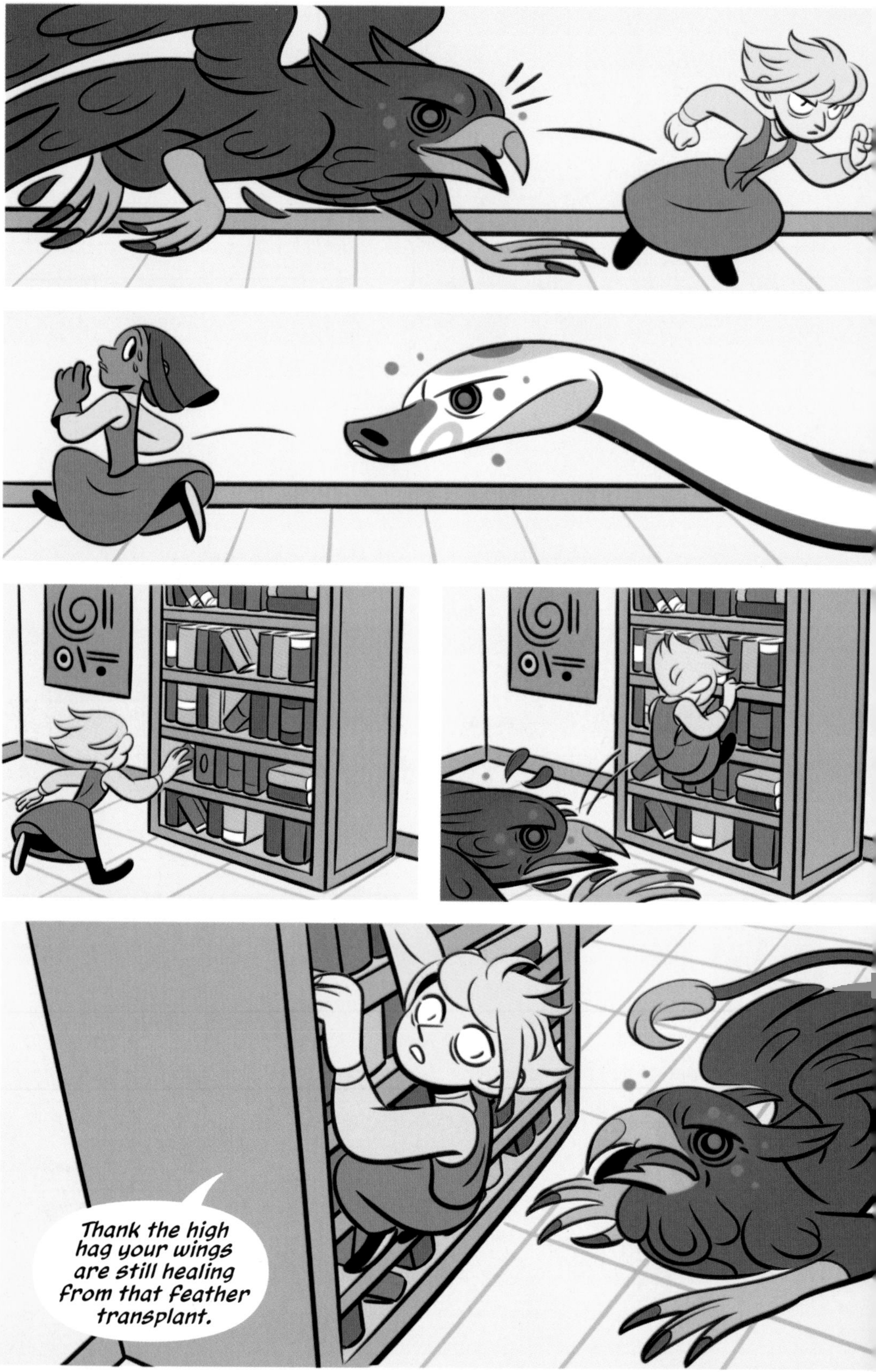
Thank the high hag your wings are still healing from that feather transplant.

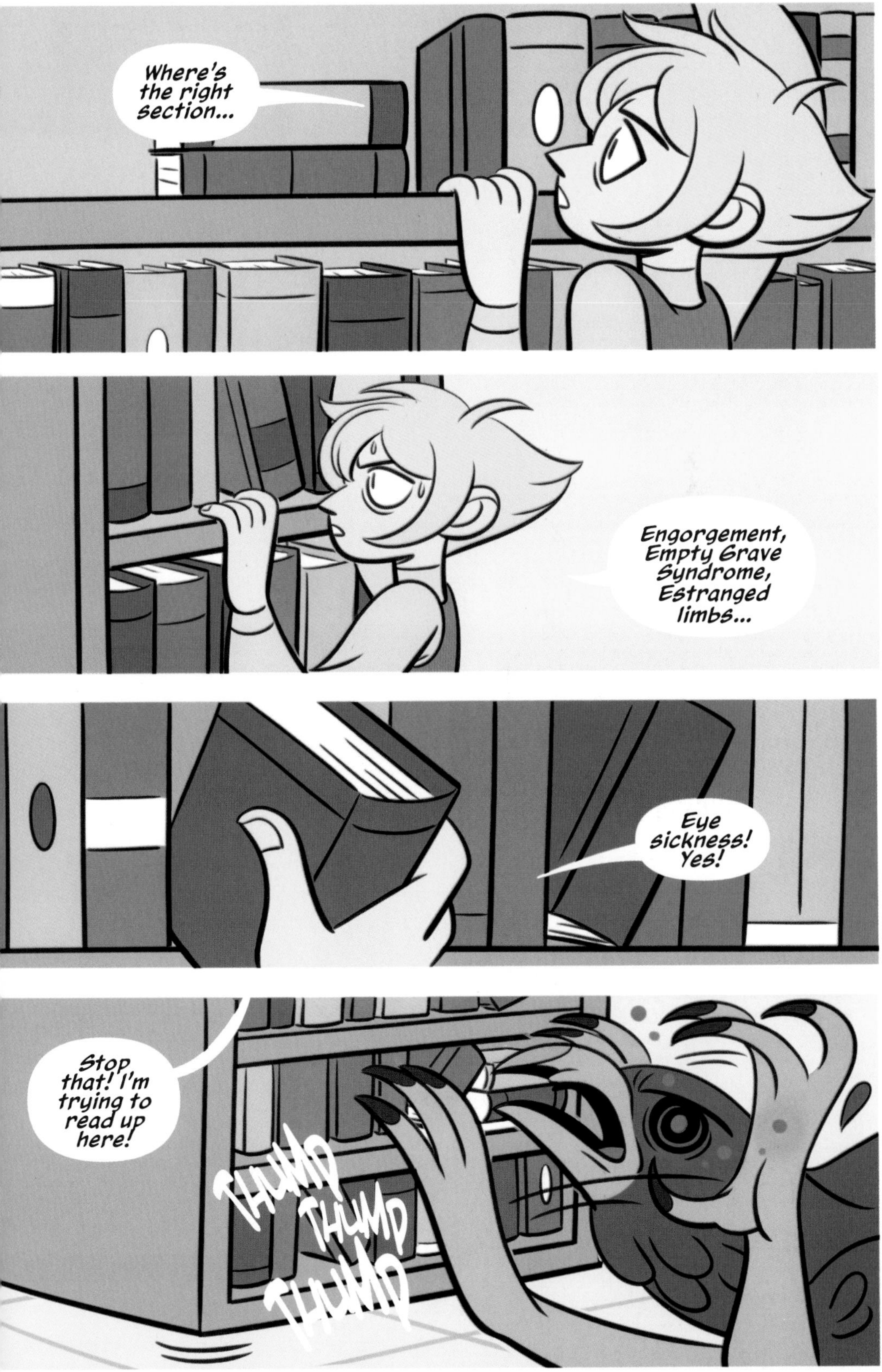
Where's the right section...
Engorgement, Empty Grave Syndrome, Estranged limbs...
Eye sickness! Yes!
Stop that! I'm trying to read up here!
THUMP THUMP THUMP

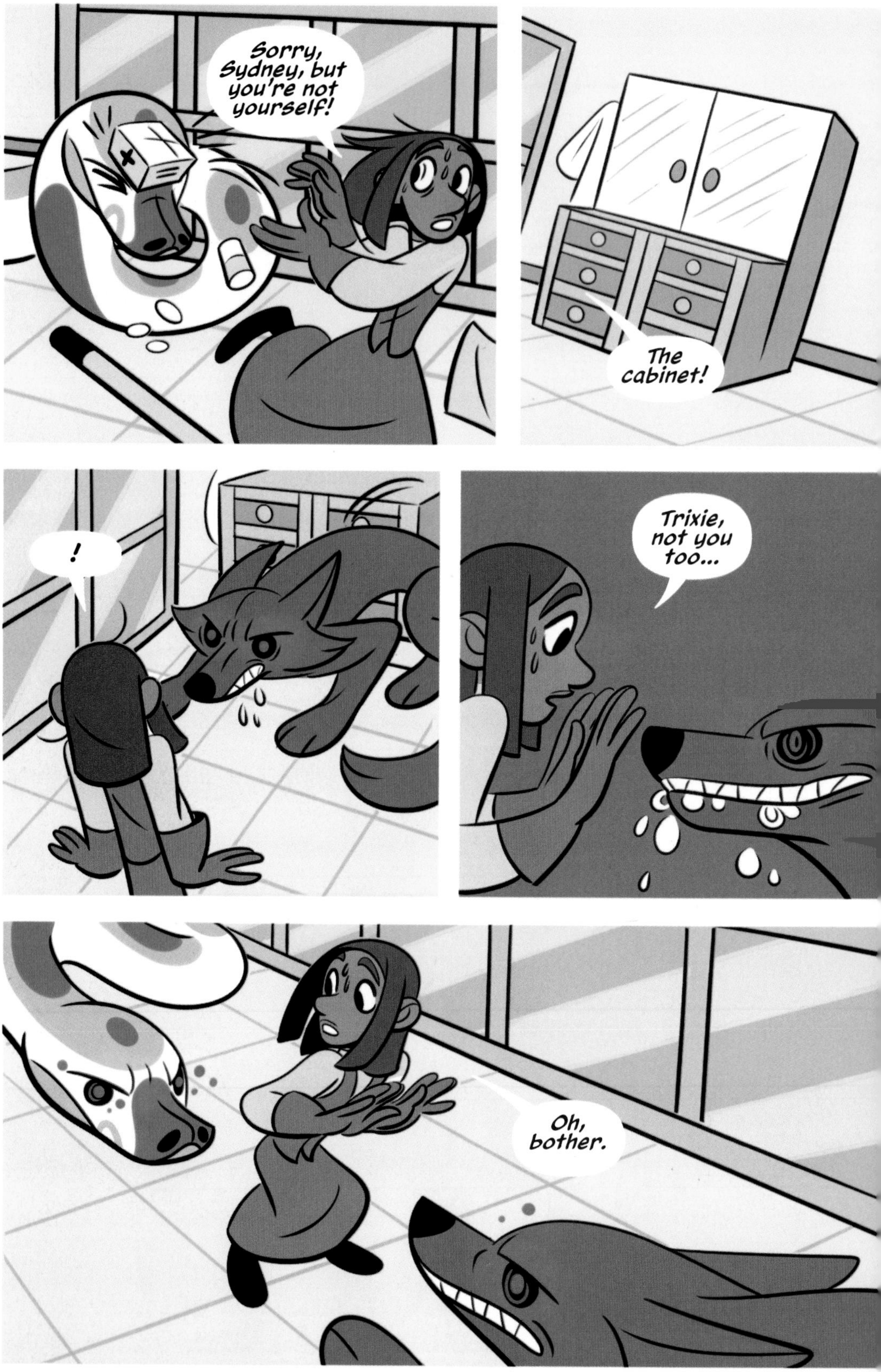

Sorry, Sydney, but you're not yourself!
The cabinet!
!
Trixie, not you too...
Oh, bother.

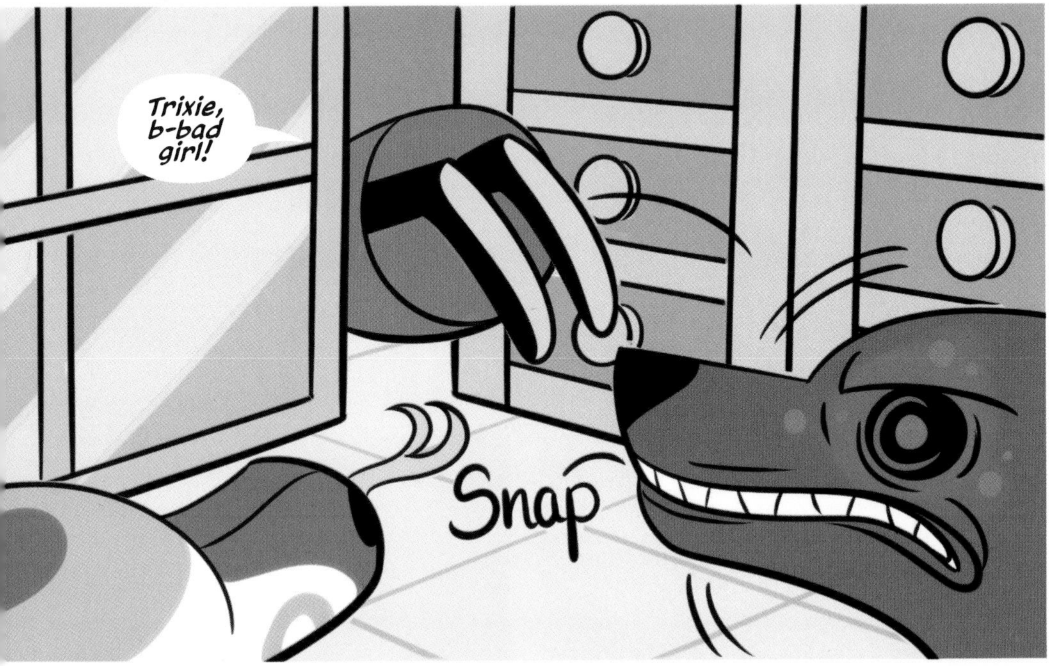
Trixie, b-bad girl!
Snap

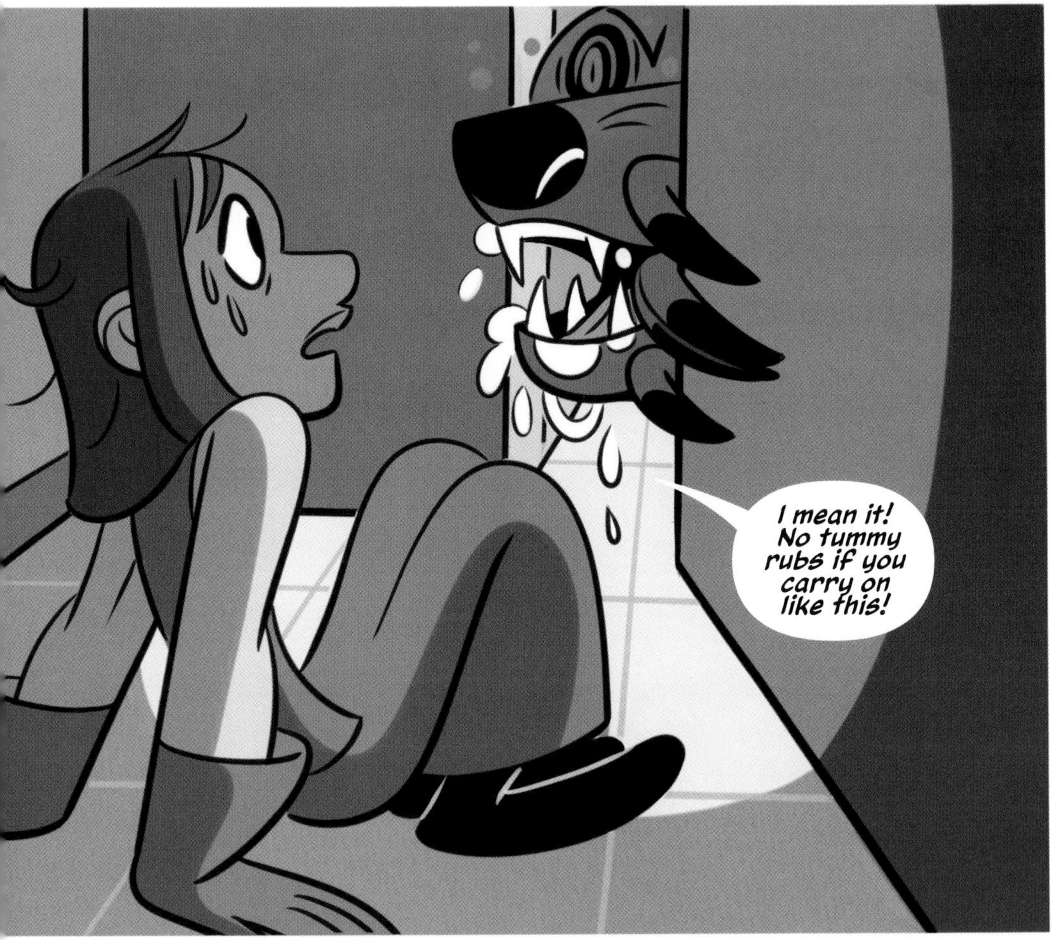
I mean it! No tummy rubs if you carry on like this!

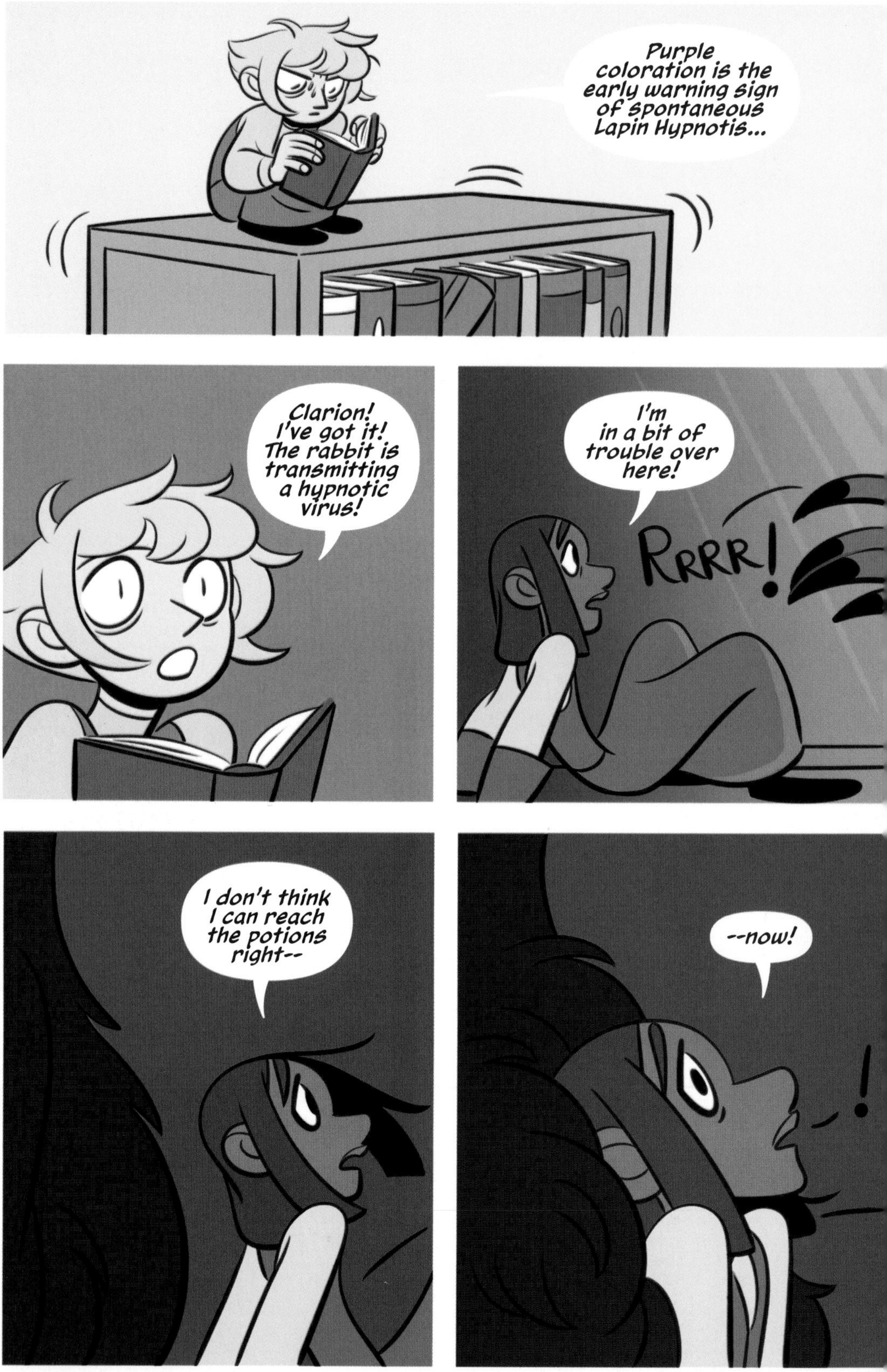
Purple coloration is the early warning sign of spontaneous Lapin Hypnotis...
Clarion! I've got it! The rabbit is transmitting a hypnotic virus!
I'm in a bit of trouble over here!
RRRR!
I don't think I can reach the potions right--
--now!

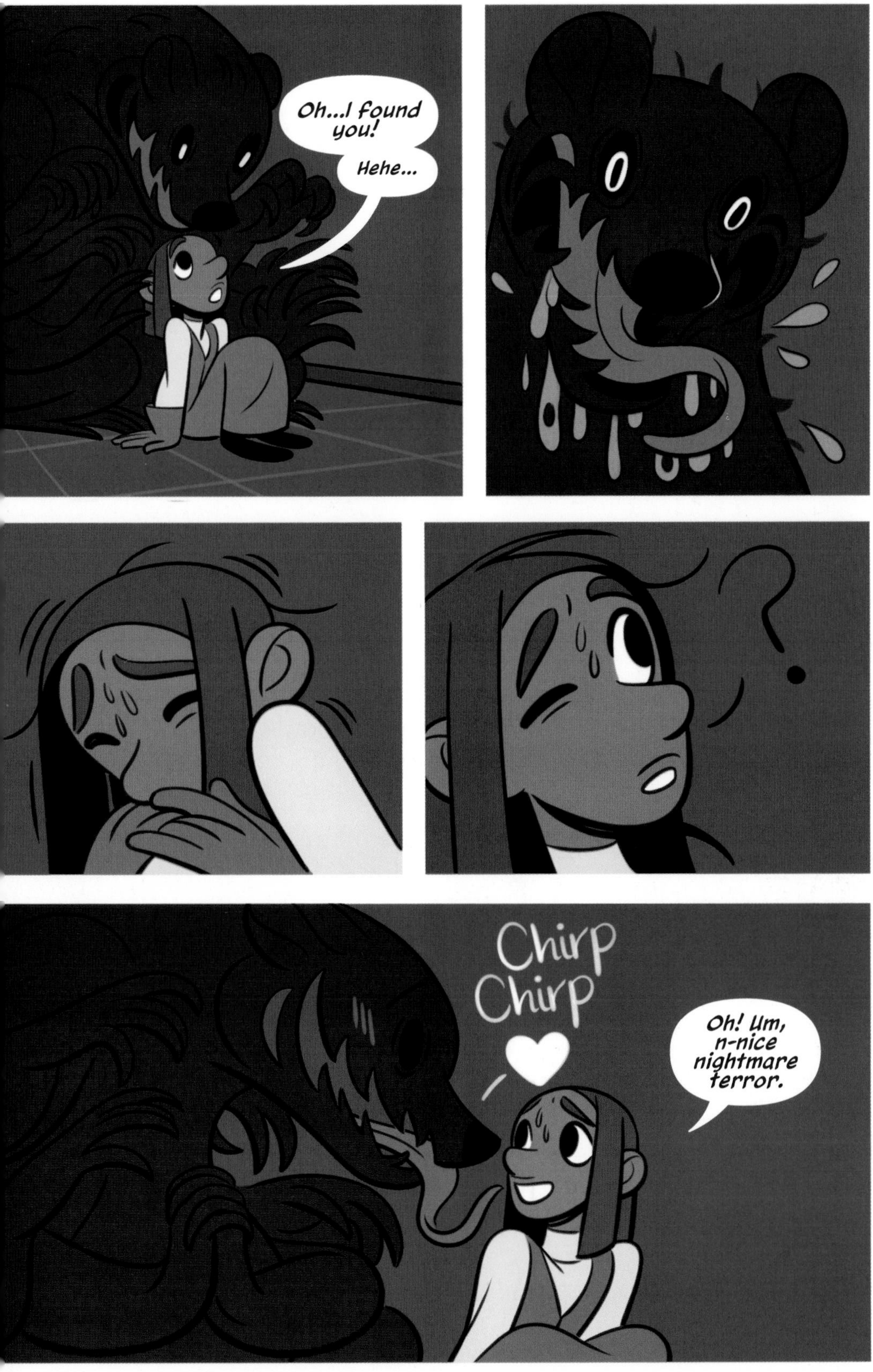
Oh...I found you!
Hehe...
Chirp
Chirp
Oh! Um, n-nice nightmare terror.

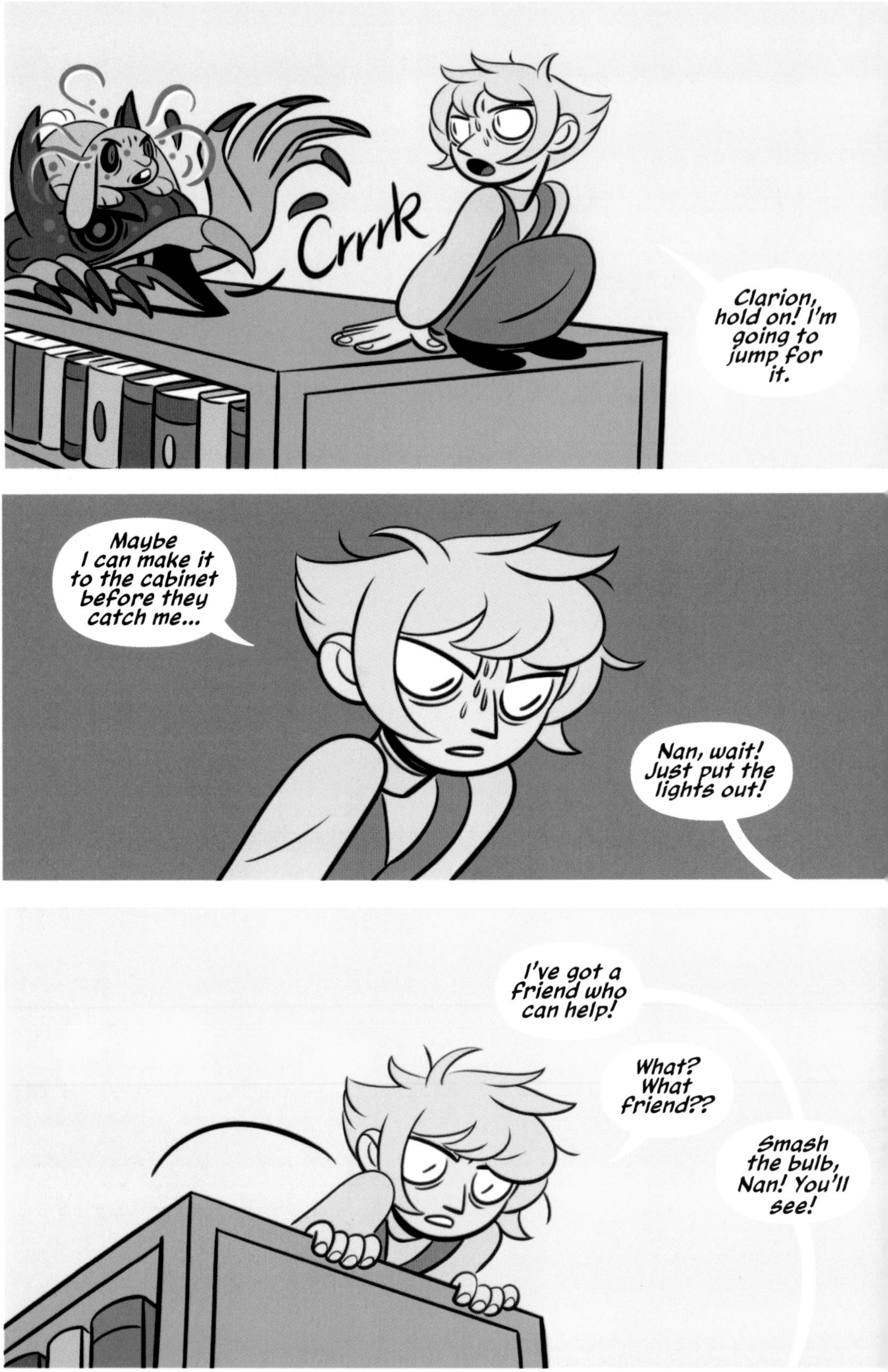
Crrrk
Clarion, hold on! I'm going to jump for it.
Maybe I can make it to the cabinet before they catch me...
Nan, wait! Just put the lights out!
I've got a friend who can help!
What? What friend??
Smash the bulb, Nan! You'll see!

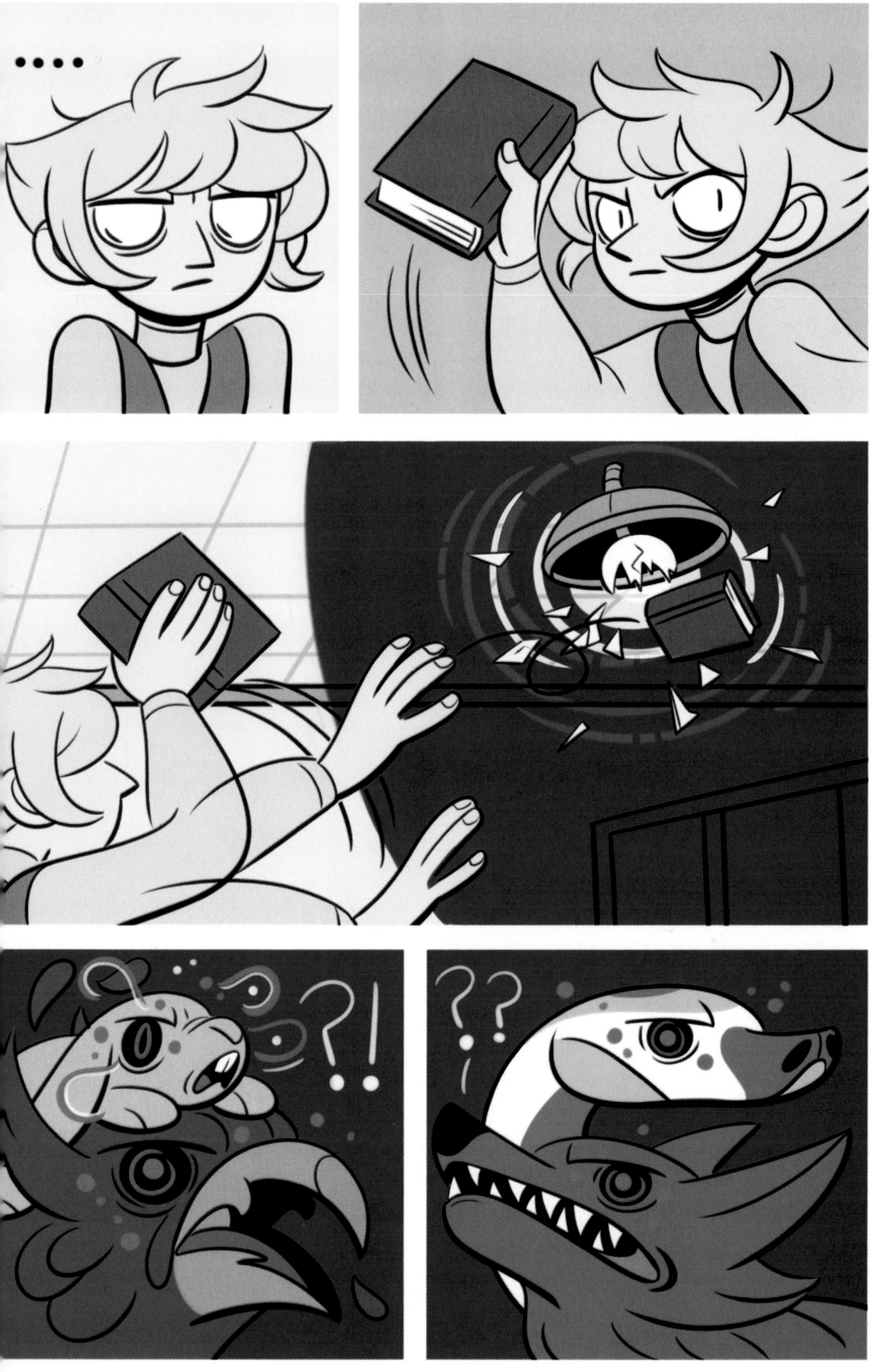
....
?!
??

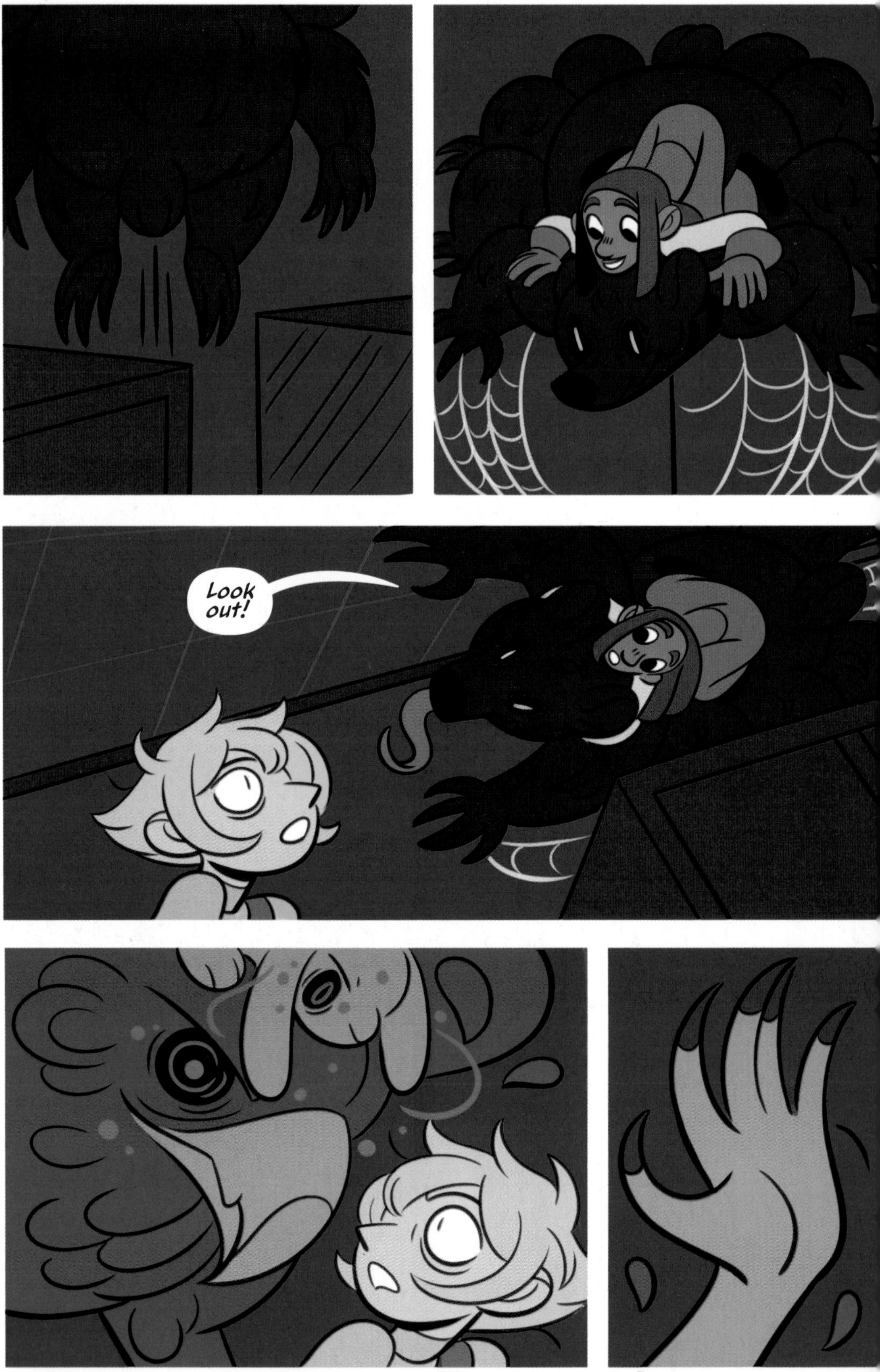
Look out!

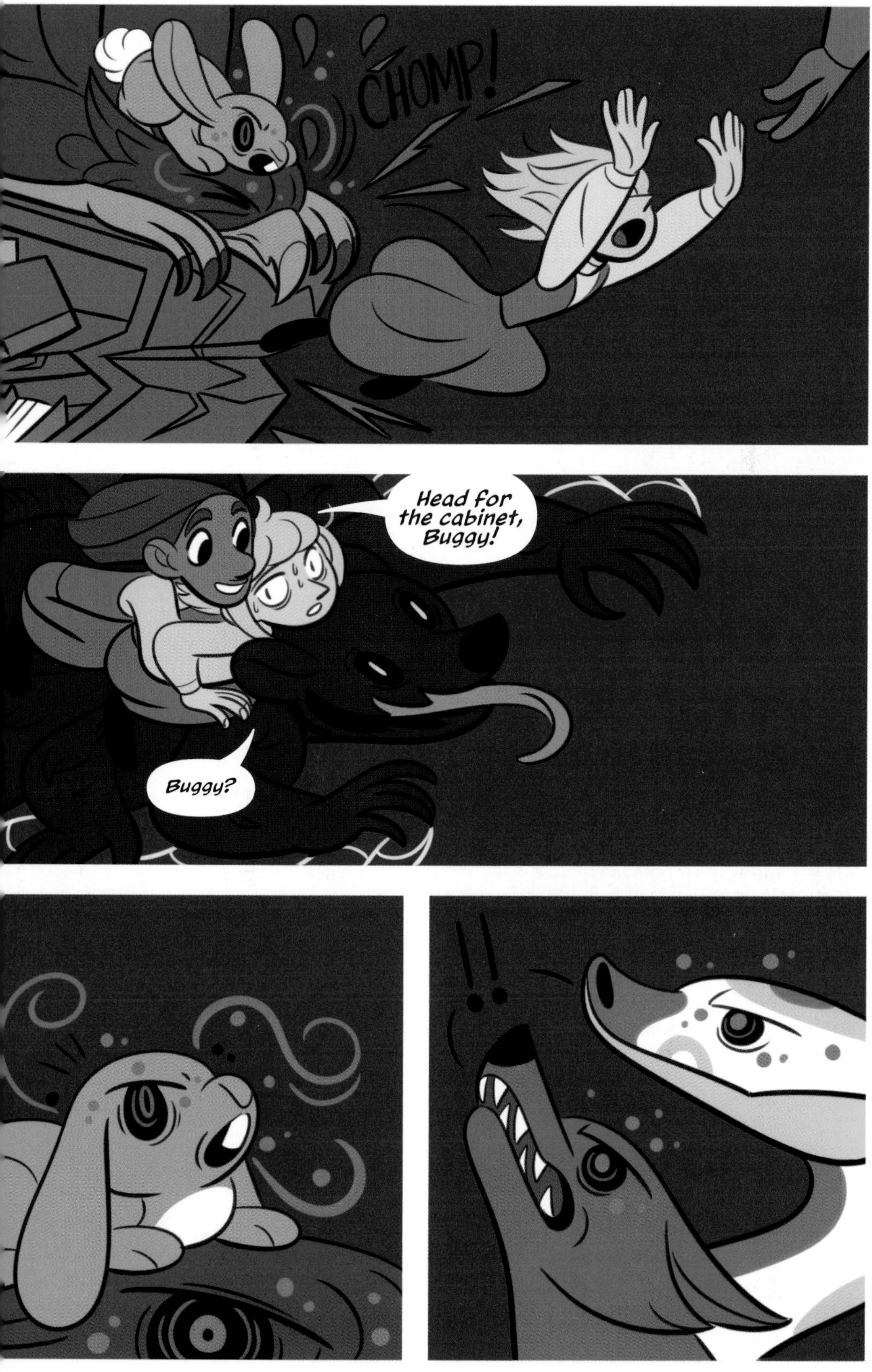
CHOMP!
Head for the cabinet, Buggy!
Buggy?
!!

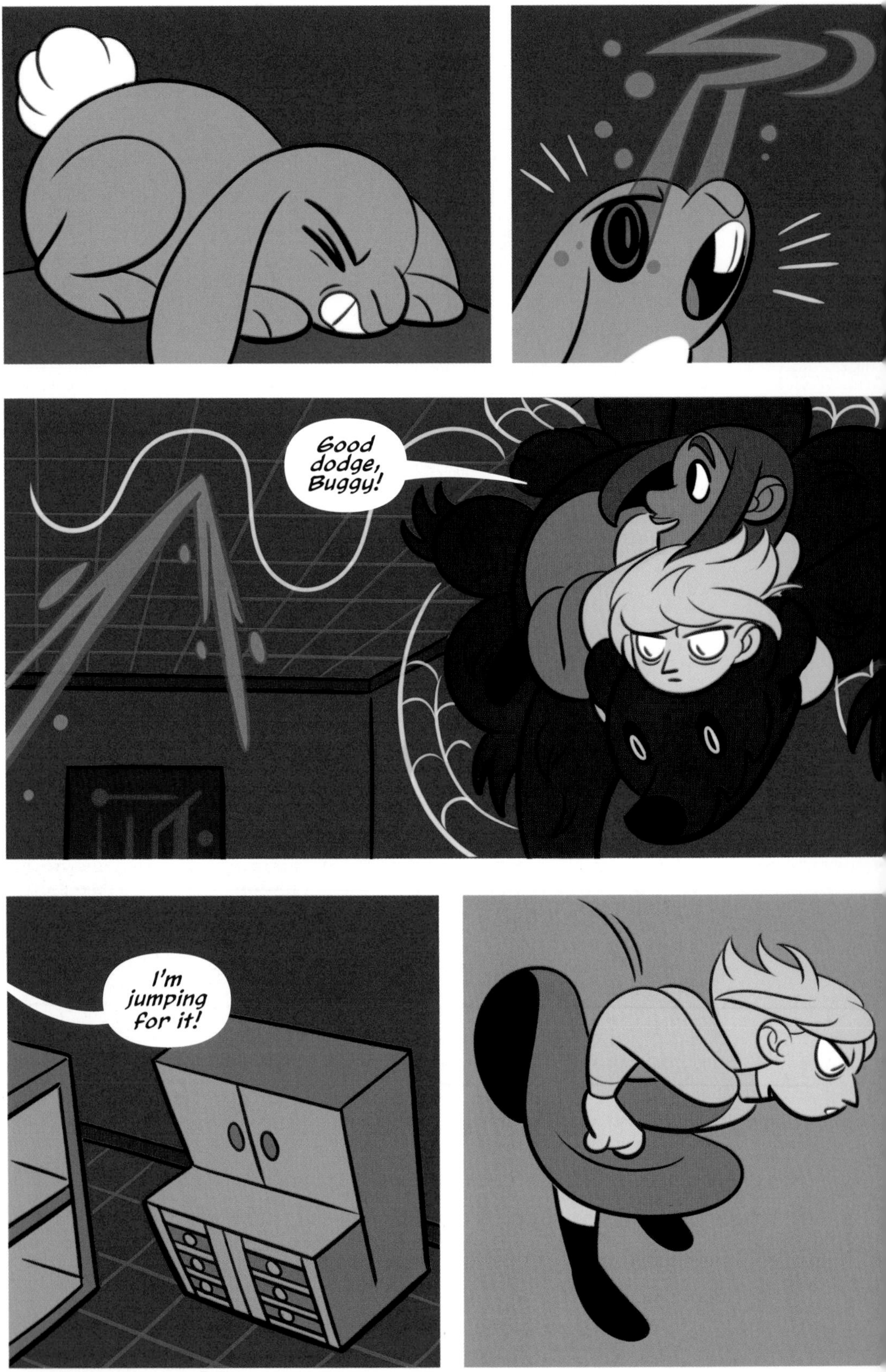
Good dodge, Buggy!
I'm jumping for it!

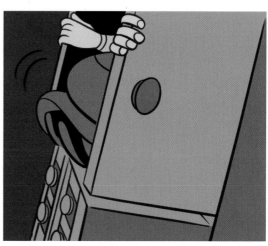

HSSS

Squirt
Squirt

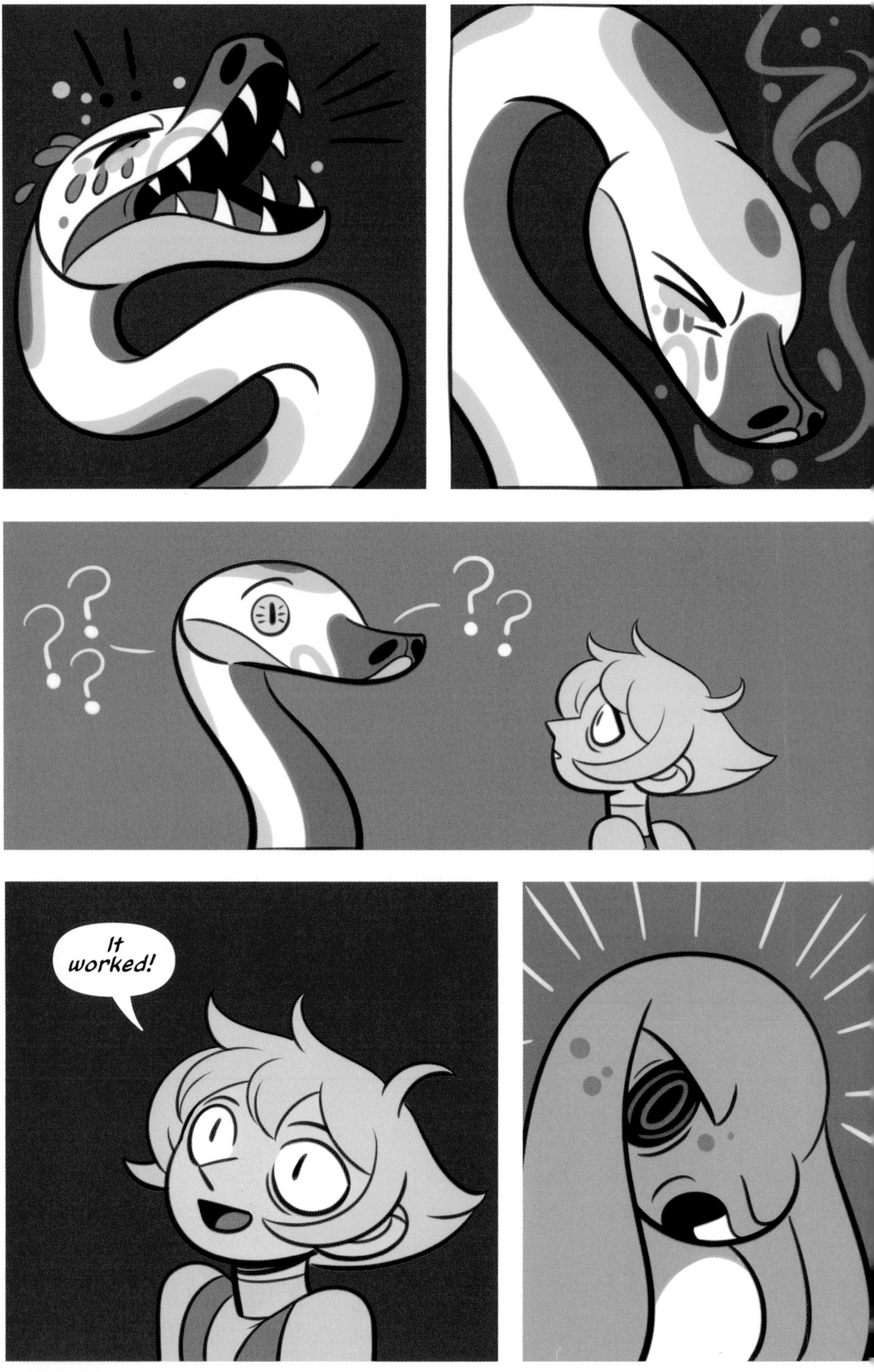
It worked!

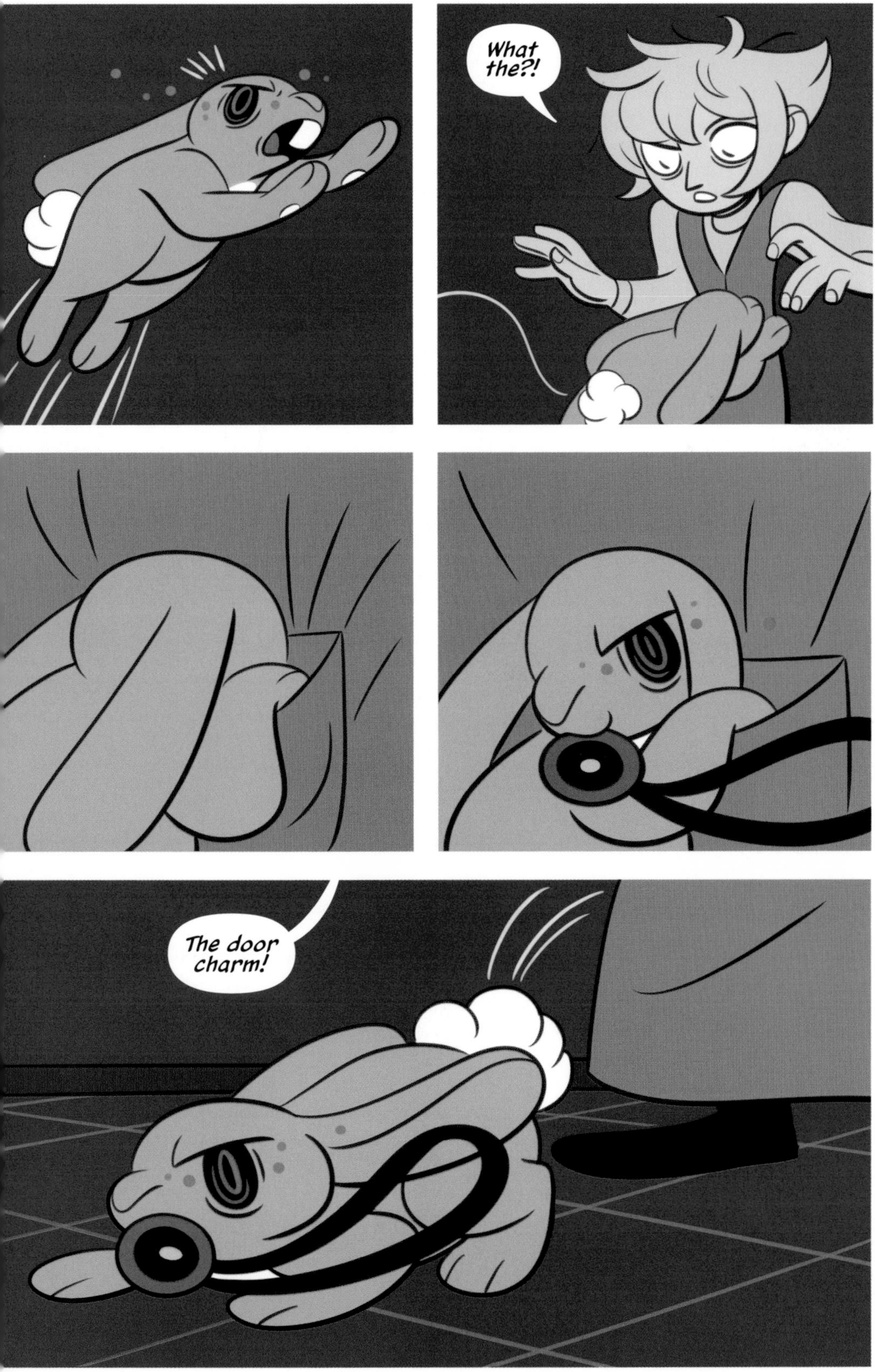
What the?!
The door charm!

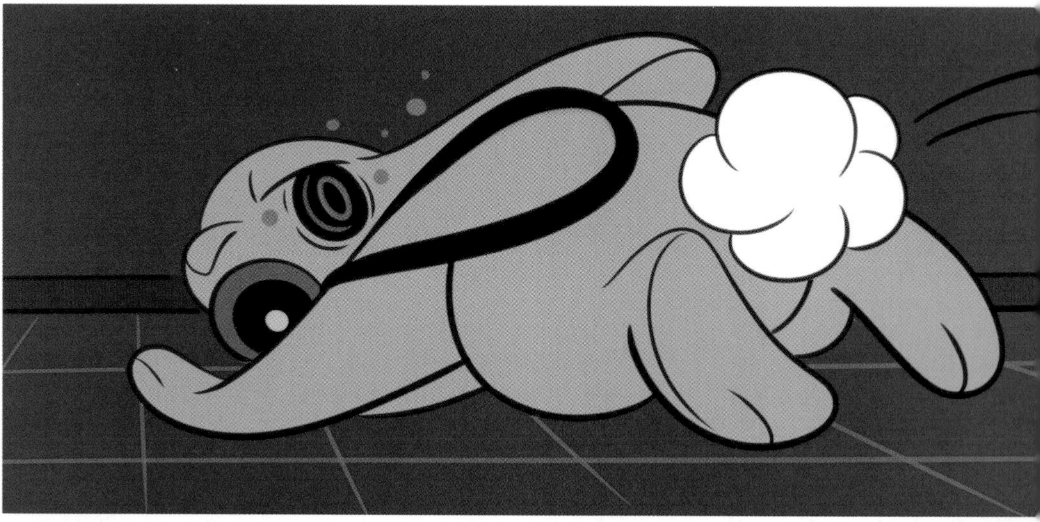

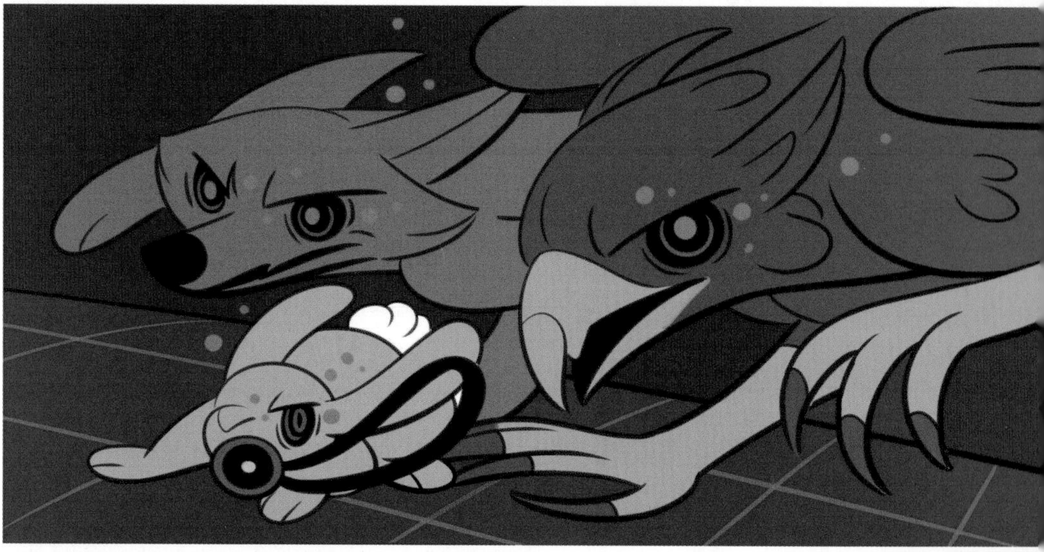

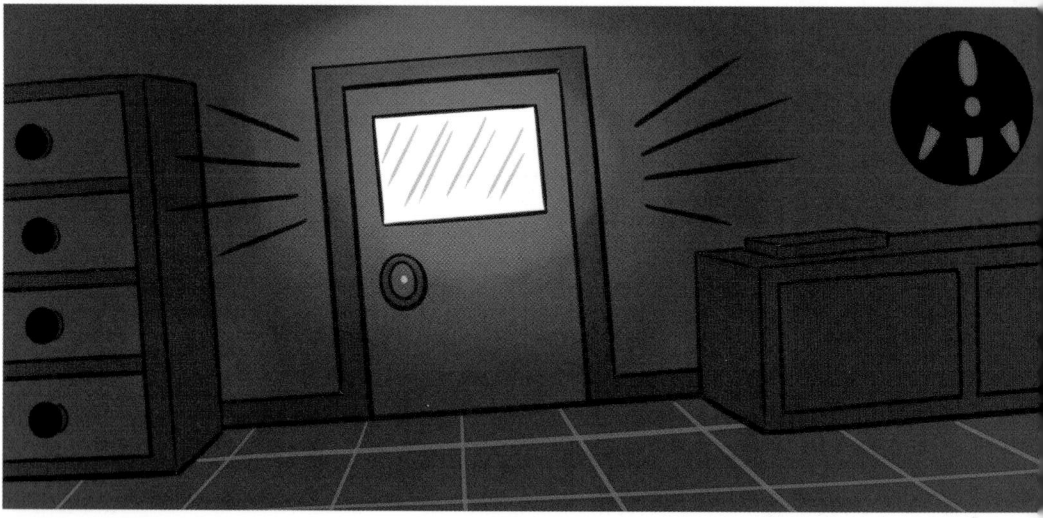

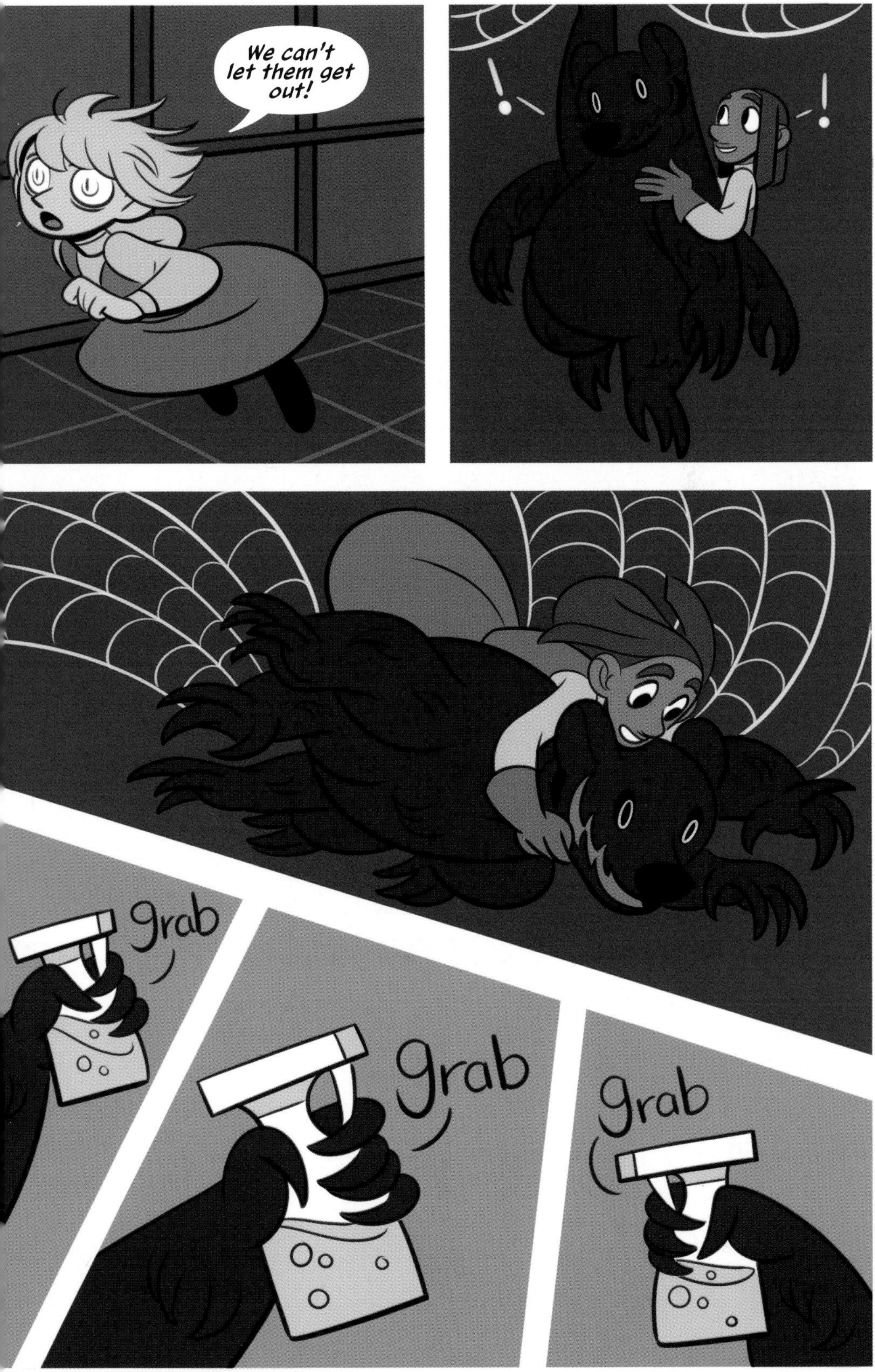
We can't let them get out!
!
!
grab
grab
grab

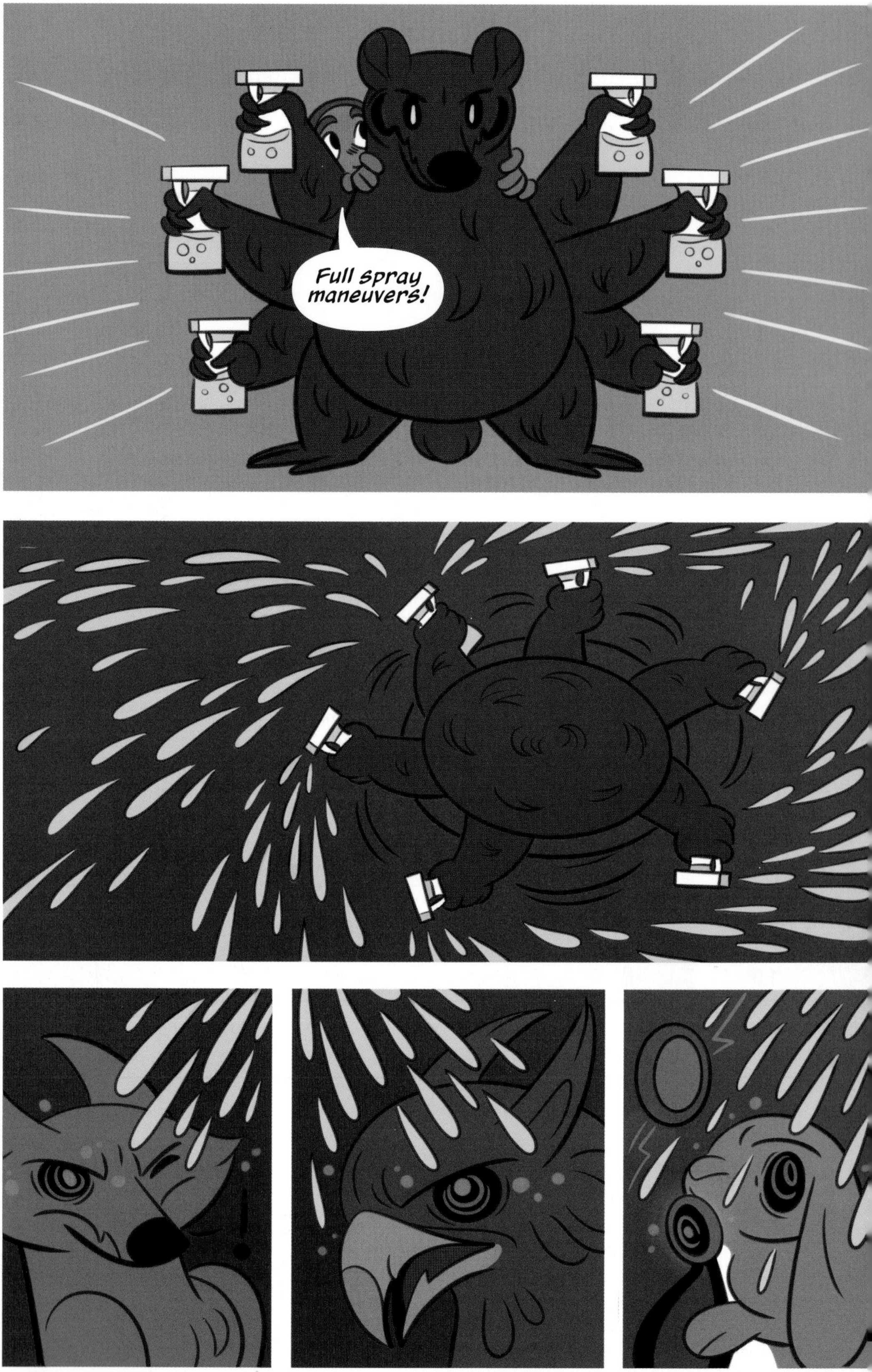
Full spray maneuvers!

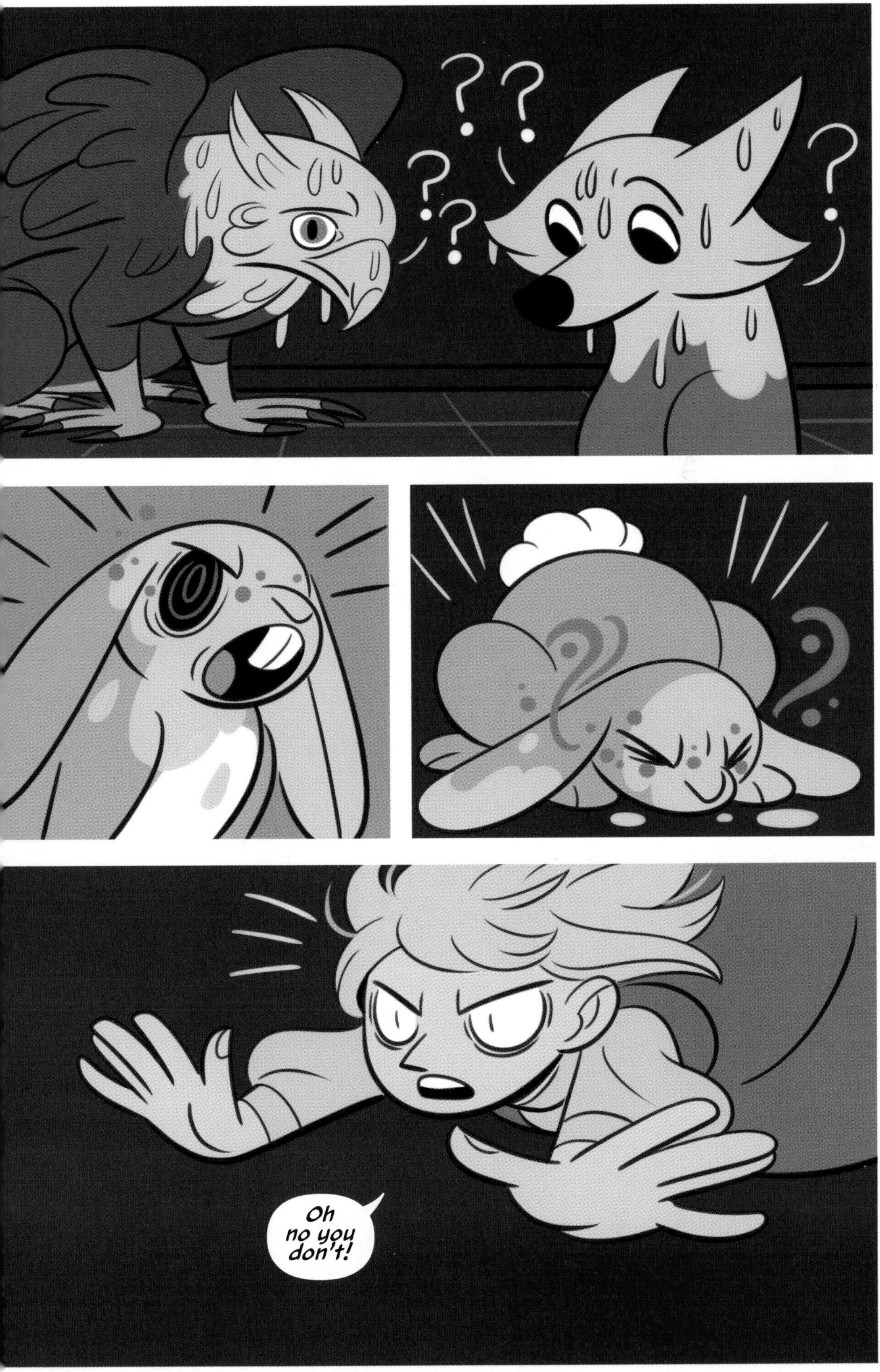
Oh no you don't!

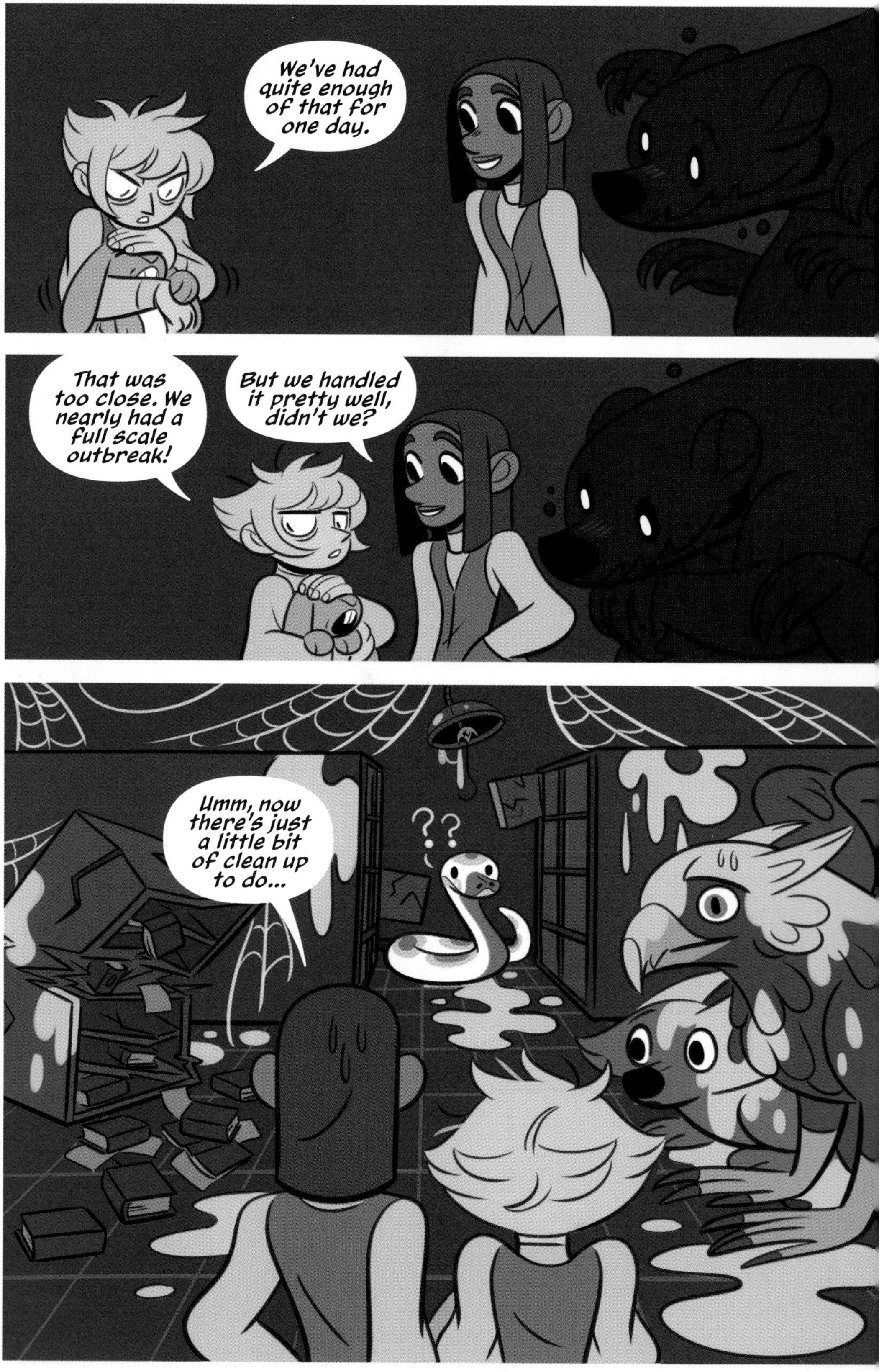
We've had quite enough of that for one day.
That was too close. We nearly had a full scale outbreak!
But we handled it pretty well, didn't we?
??
Umm, now there's just a little bit of clean up to do...

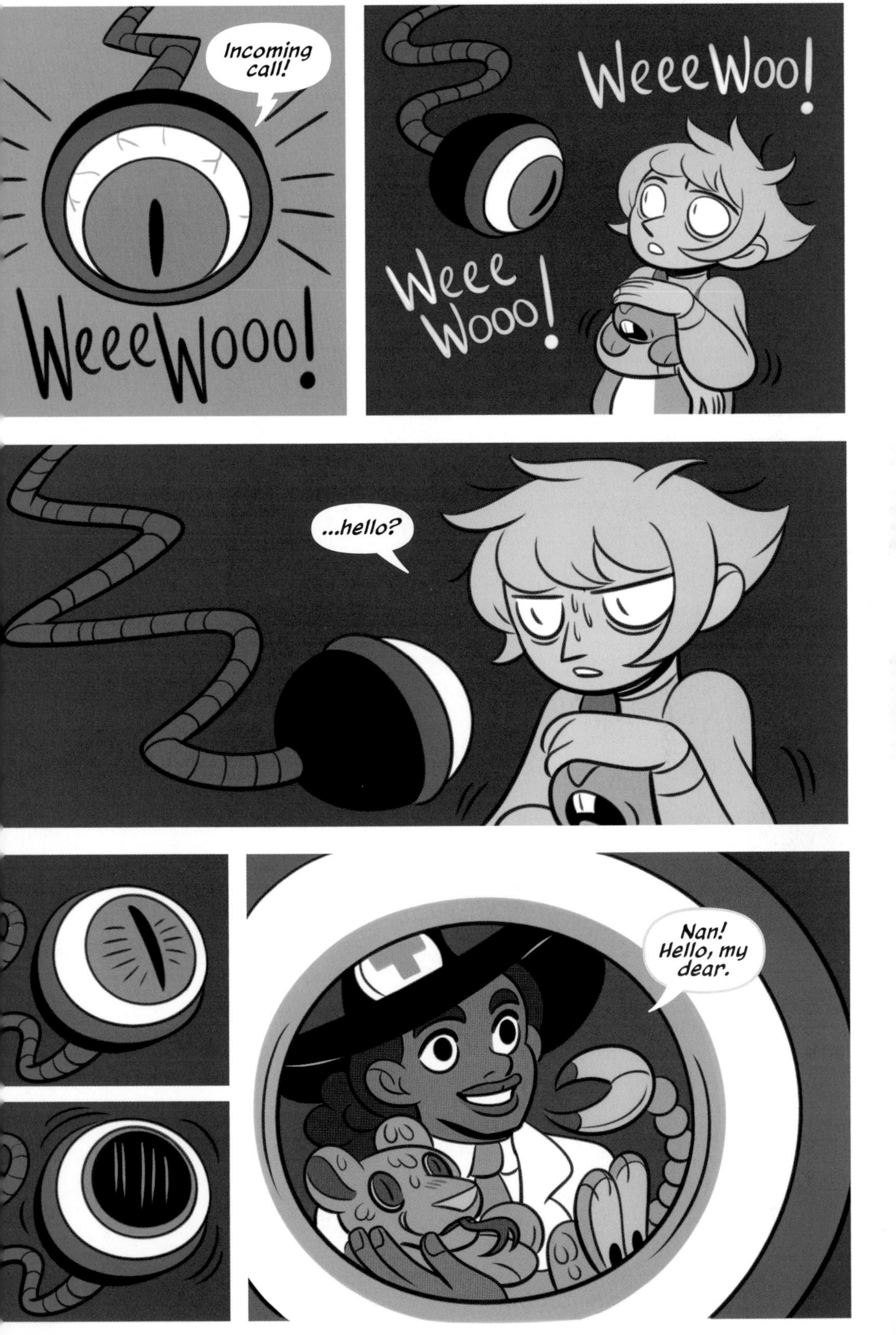
Incoming call!
WeeeWooo!
WeeeWoo!
Weee Wooo!
...hello?
Nan! Hello, my dear.

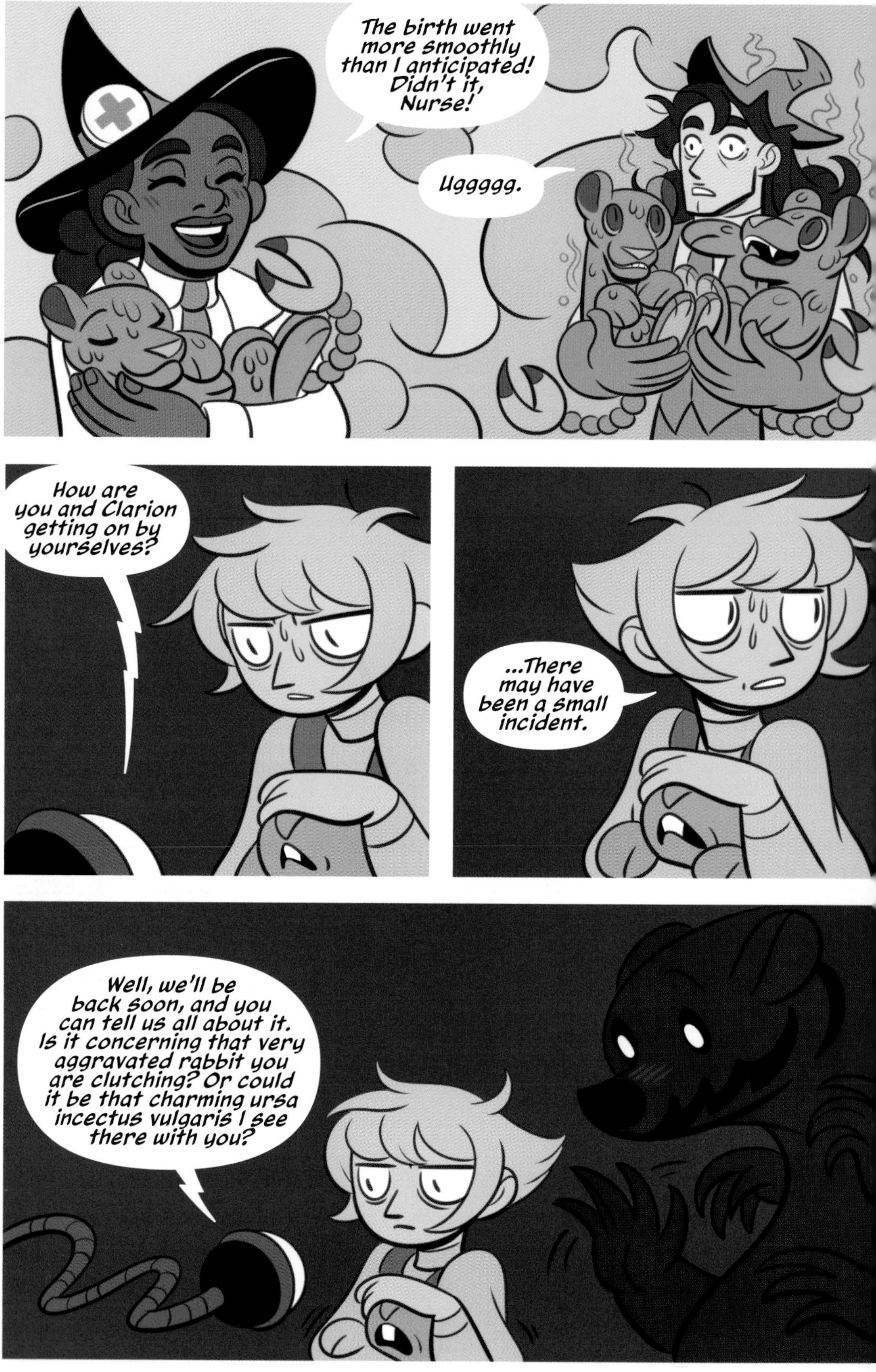
The birth went more smoothly than I anticipated! Didn't it, Nurse!
Uggggg.
How are you and Clarion getting on by yourselves?
...There may have been a small incident.
Well, we'll be back soon, and you can tell us all about it. Is it concerning that very aggravated rabbit you are clutching? Or could it be that charming ursa incectus vulgaris I see there with you?

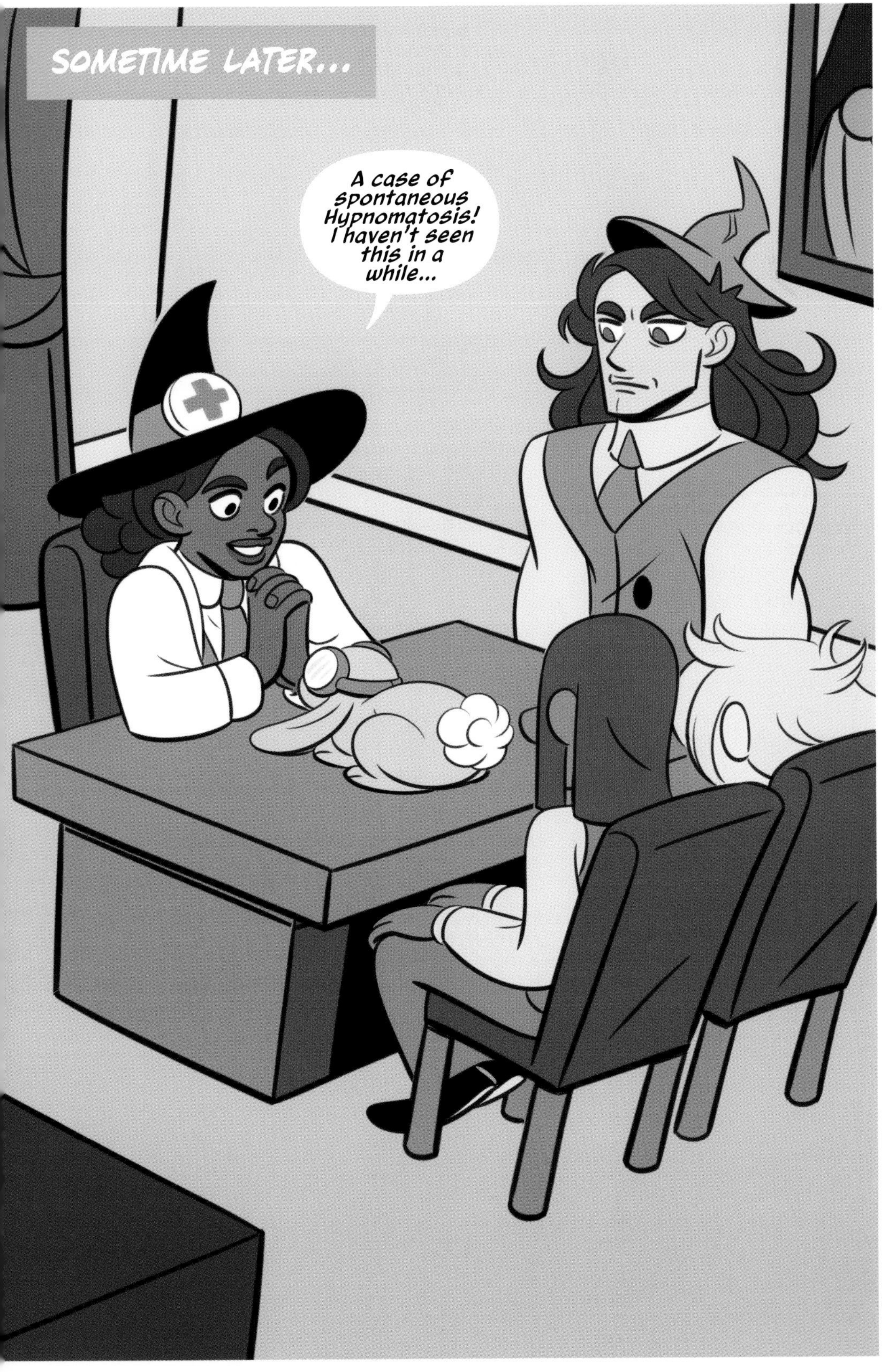
SOMETIME LATER...
A case of spontaneous Hypnomatosis! I haven't seen this in a while...

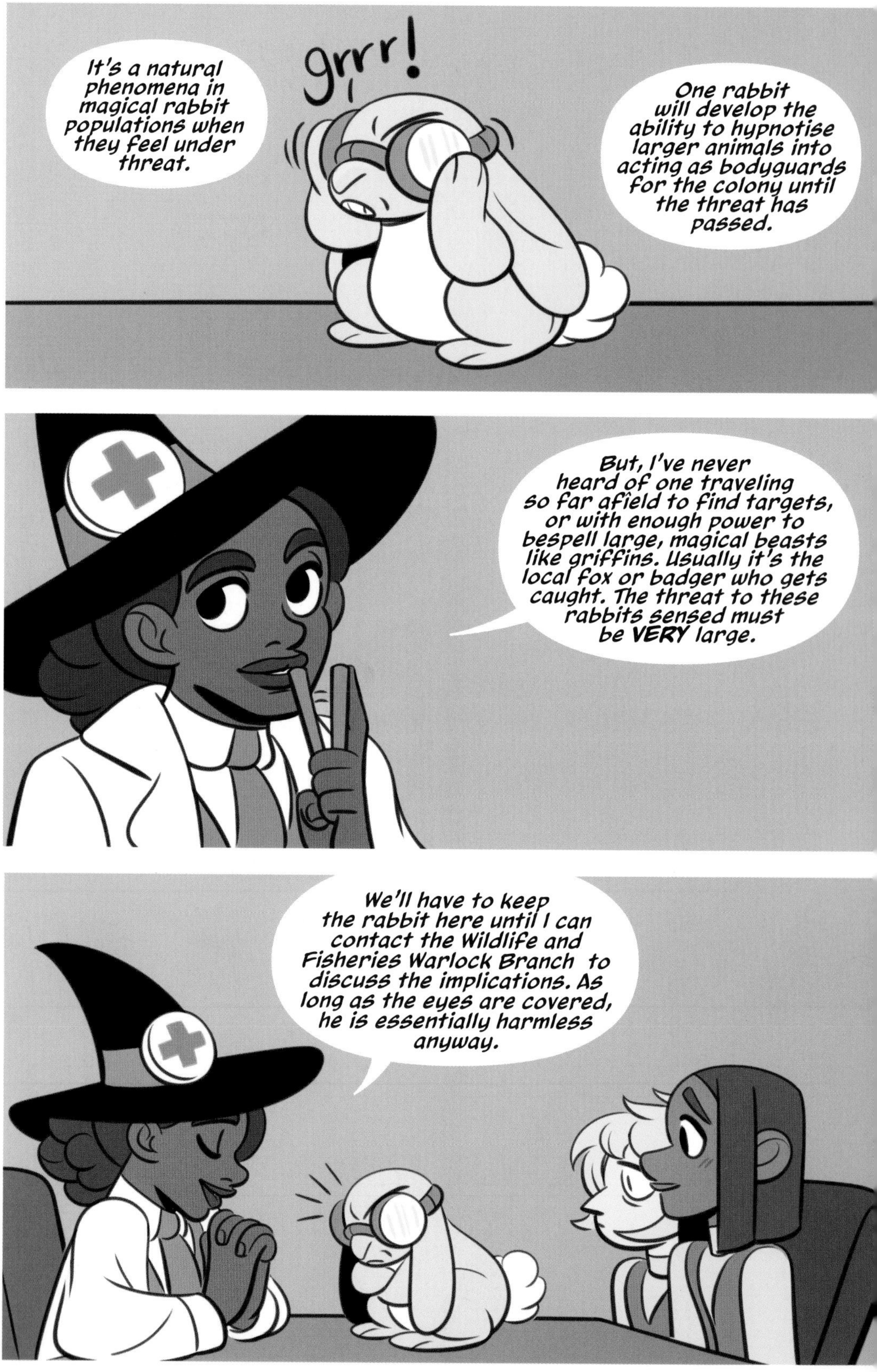

It's a natural phenomena in magical rabbit populations when they feel under threat.
grrr!
One rabbit will develop the ability to hypnotise larger animals into acting as bodyguards for the colony until the threat has passed.
But, I've never heard of one traveling so far afield to find targets, or with enough power to bespell large, magical beasts like griffins. Usually it's the local fox or badger who gets caught. The threat to these rabbits sensed must be **VERY** large.
We'll have to keep the rabbit here until I can contact the Wildlife and Fisheries Warlock Branch to discuss the implications. As long as the eyes are covered, he is essentially harmless anyway.

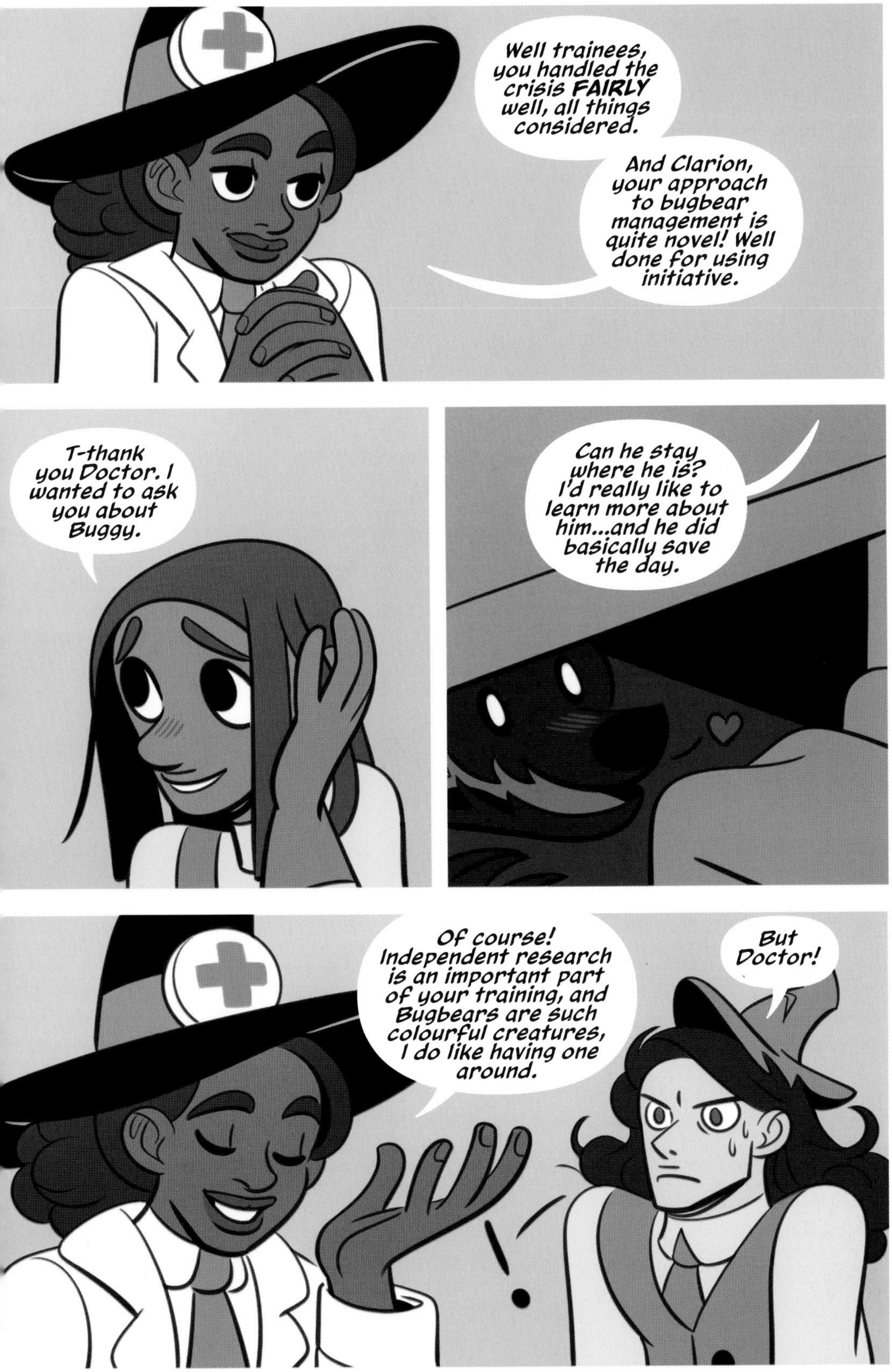
Well trainees, you handled the crisis FAIRLY well, all things considered.
And Clarion, your approach to bugbear management is quite novel! Well done for using initiative.
T-thank you Doctor. I wanted to ask you about Buggy.
Can he stay where he is? I'd really like to learn more about him...and he did basically save the day.
Of course! Independent research is an important part of your training, and Bugbears are such colourful creatures, I do like having one around.
But Doctor!

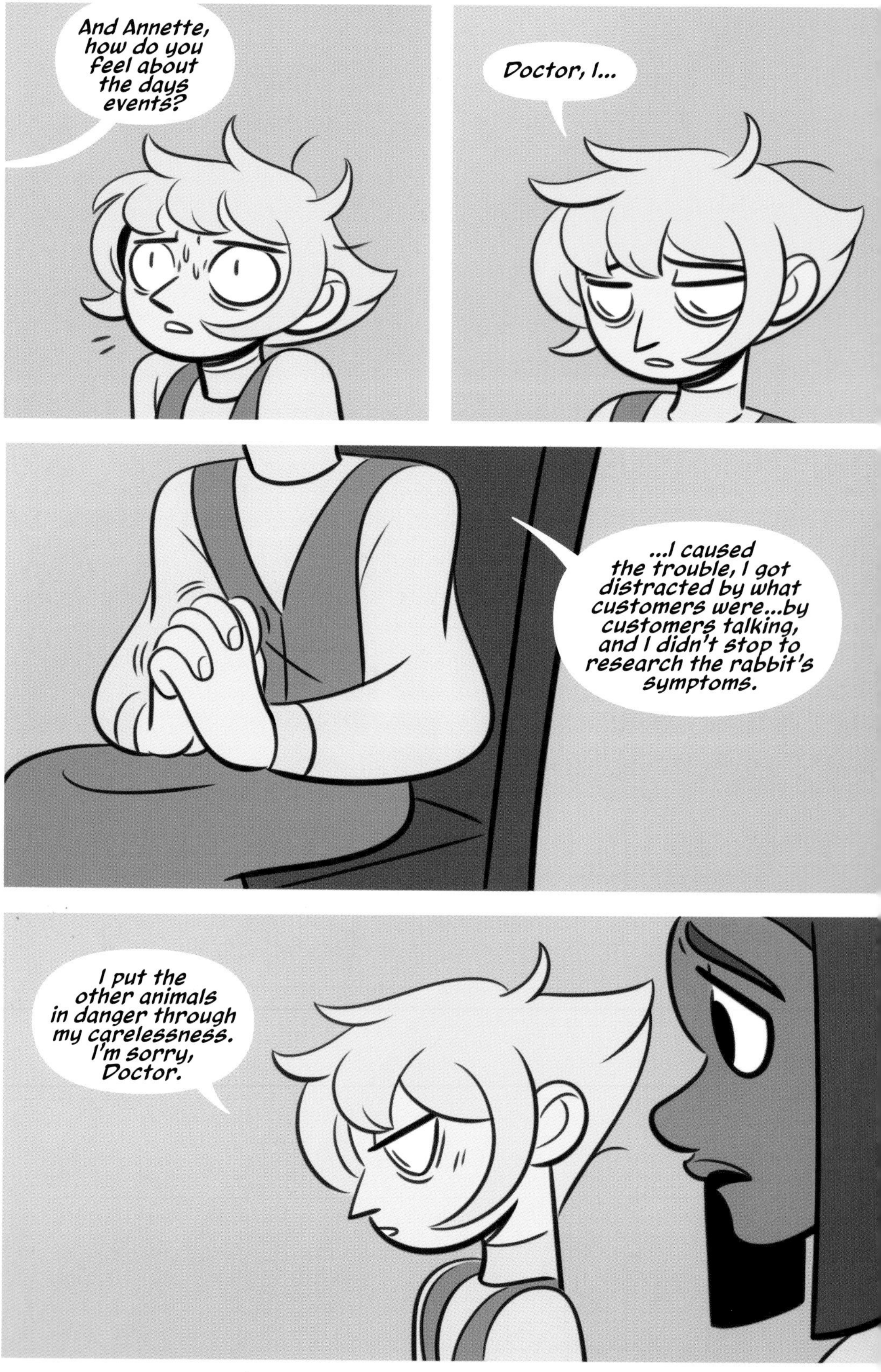

And Annette, how do you feel about the days events?
Doctor, I...
...I caused the trouble, I got distracted by what customers were...by customers talking, and I didn't stop to research the rabbit's symptoms.
I put the other animals in danger through my carelessness. I'm sorry, Doctor.

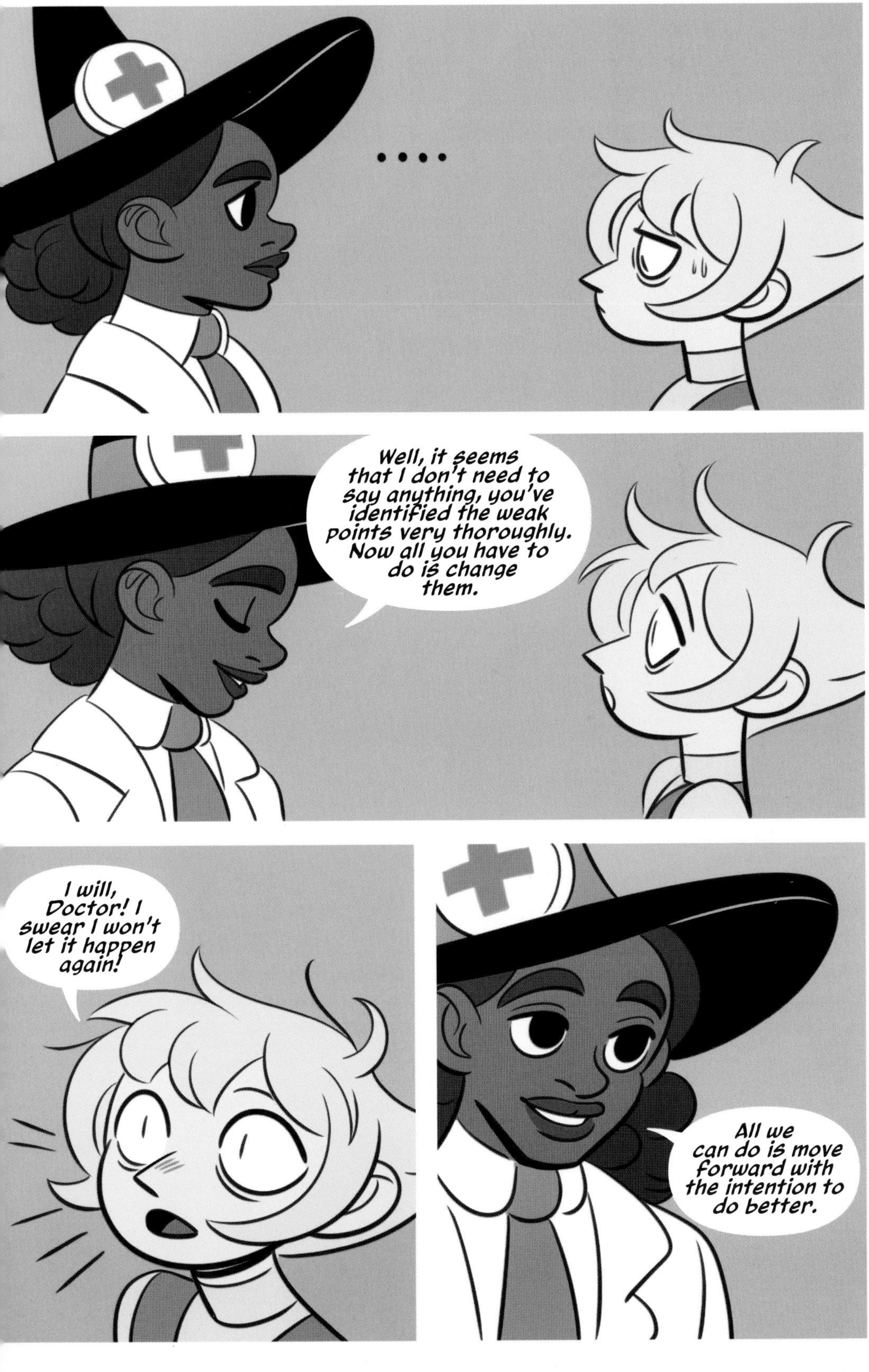
....
Well, it seems that I don't need to say anything, you've identified the weak points very thoroughly. Now all you have to do is change them.
I will, Doctor! I swear I won't let it happen again!
All we can do is move forward with the intention to do better.

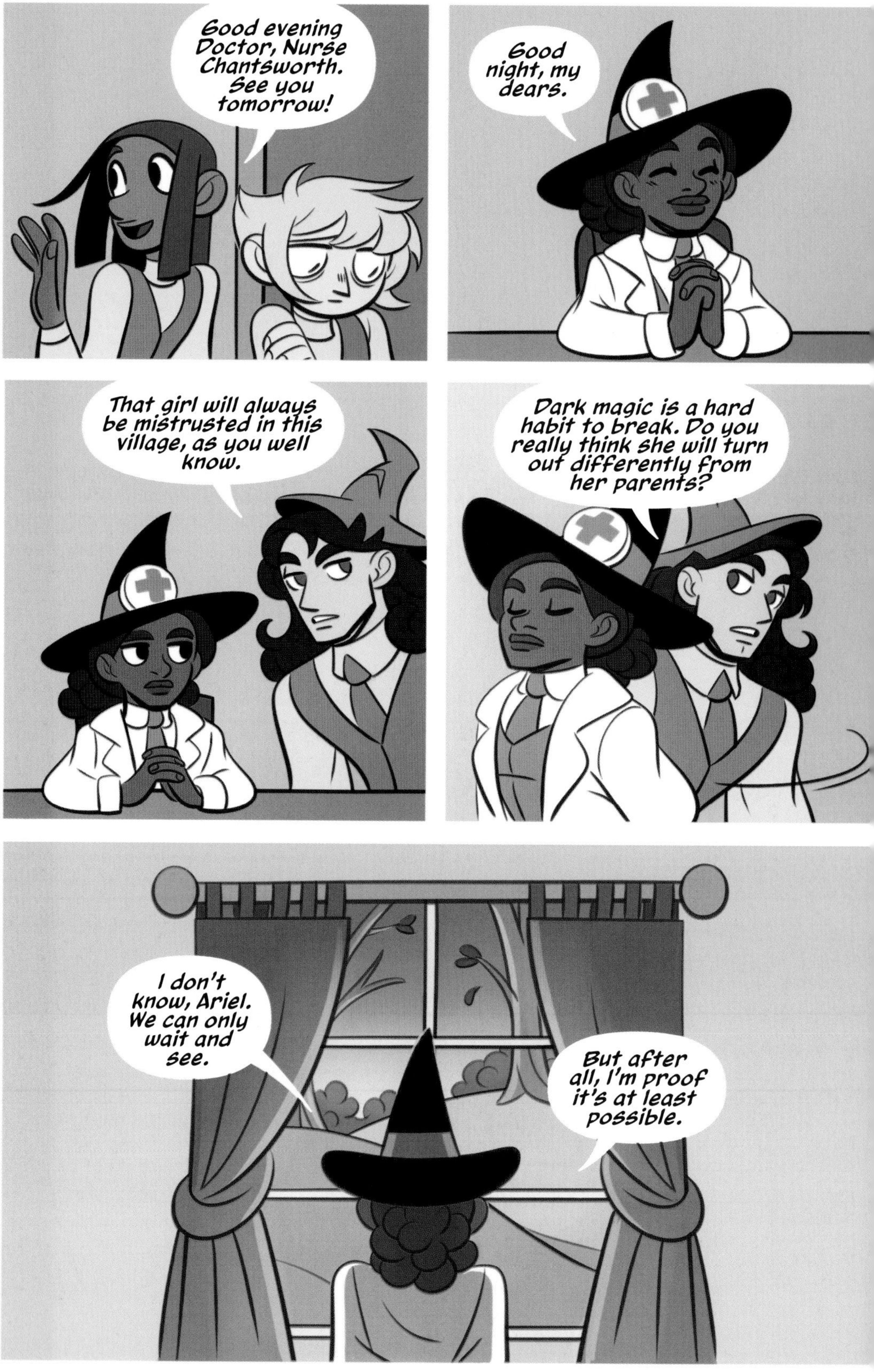
Good evening Doctor, Nurse Chantsworth. See you tomorrow!
Good night, my dears.
That girl will always be mistrusted in this village, as you well know.
Dark magic is a hard habit to break. Do you really think she will turn out differently from her parents?
I don't know, Ariel. We can only wait and see.
But after all, I'm proof it's at least possible.

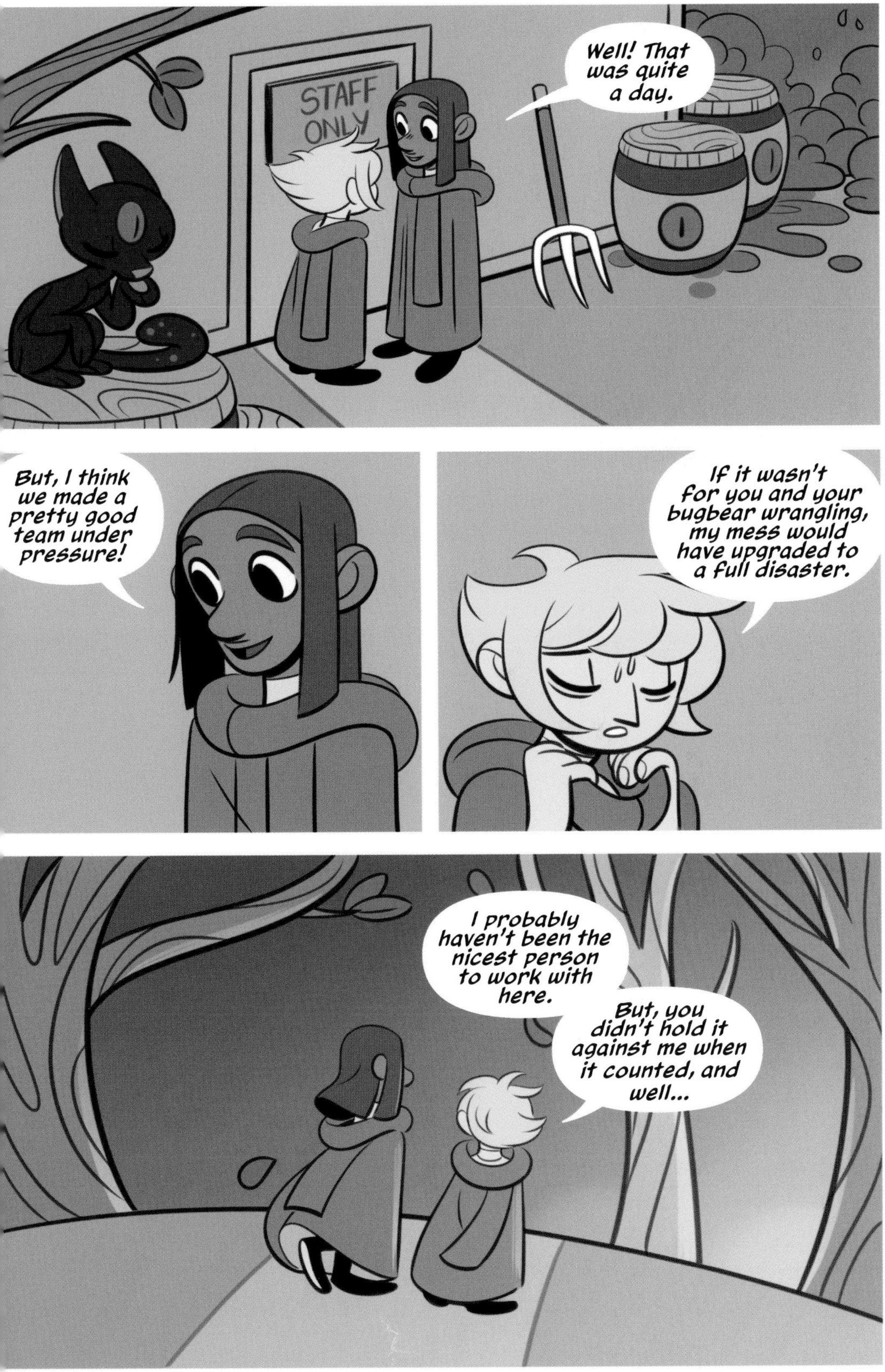
STAFF ONLY
Well! That was quite a day.
But, I think we made a pretty good team under pressure!
If it wasn't for you and your bugbear wrangling, my mess would have upgraded to a full disaster.
I probably haven't been the nicest person to work with here.
But, you didn't hold it against me when it counted, and well...

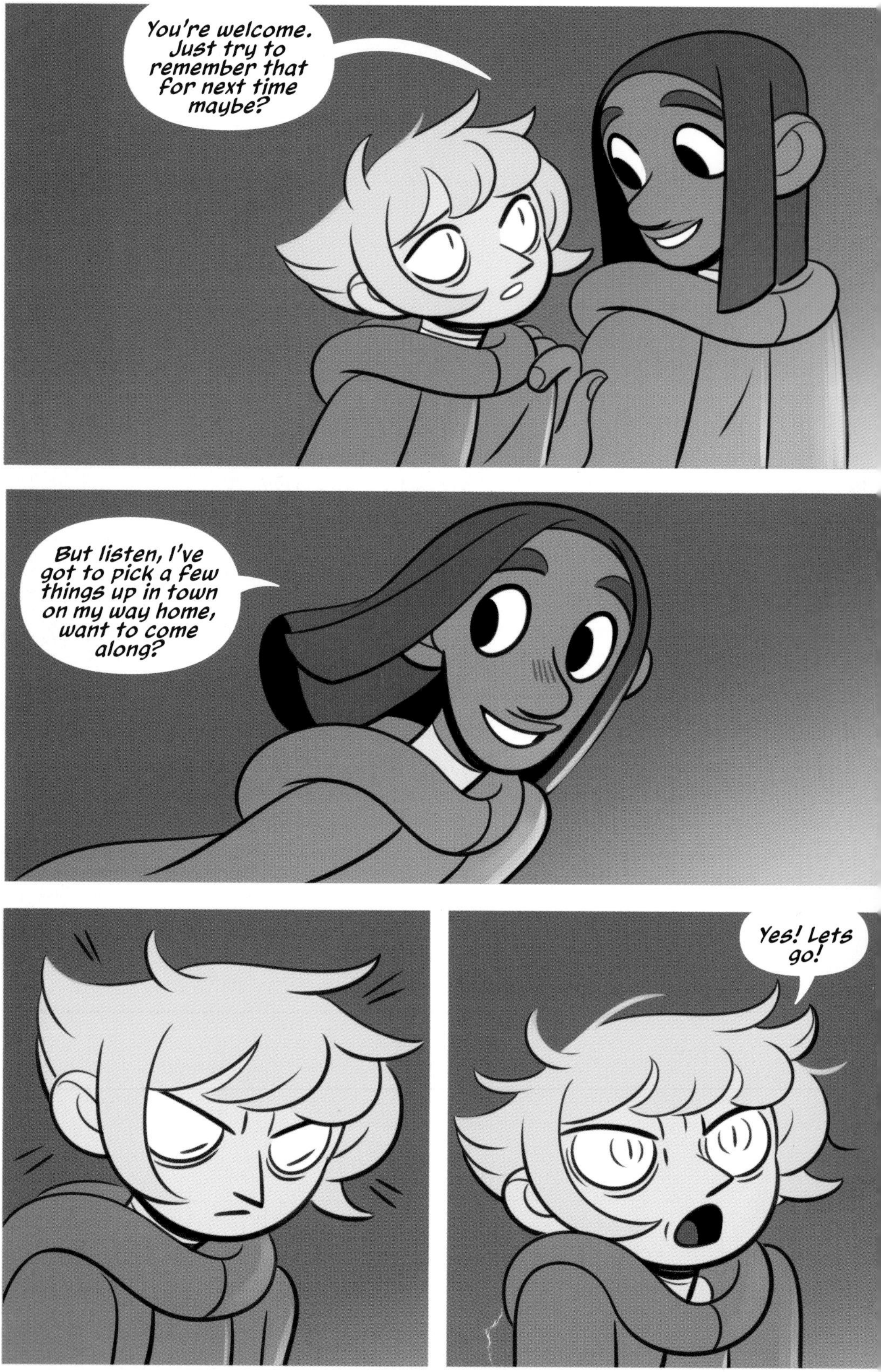
You're welcome. Just try to remember that for next time maybe?
But listen, I've got to pick a few things up in town on my way home, want to come along?
Yes! Lets go!

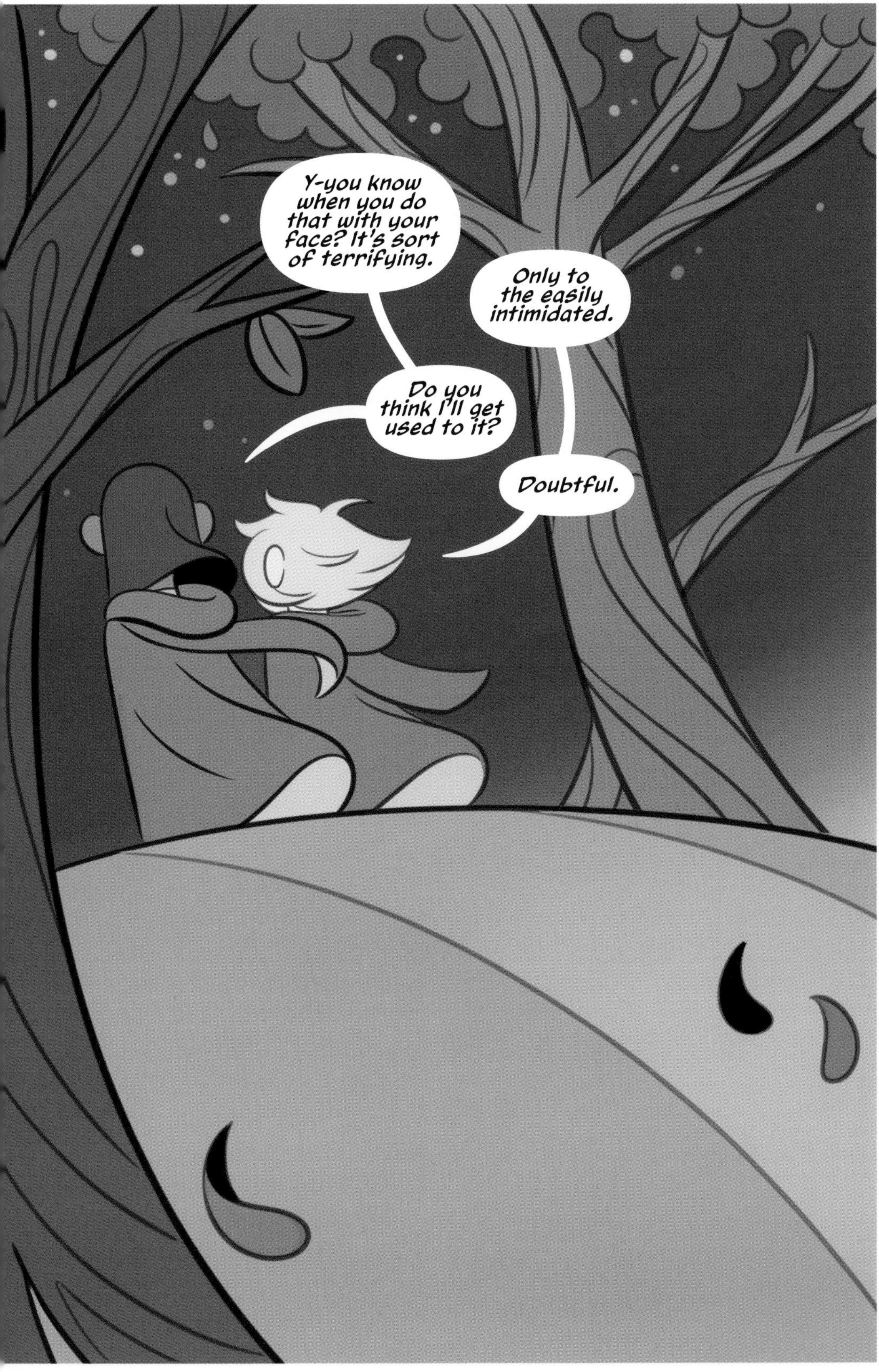
Y-you know when you do that with your face? It's sort of terrifying.
Only to the easily intimidated.
Do you think I'll get used to it?
Doubtful.

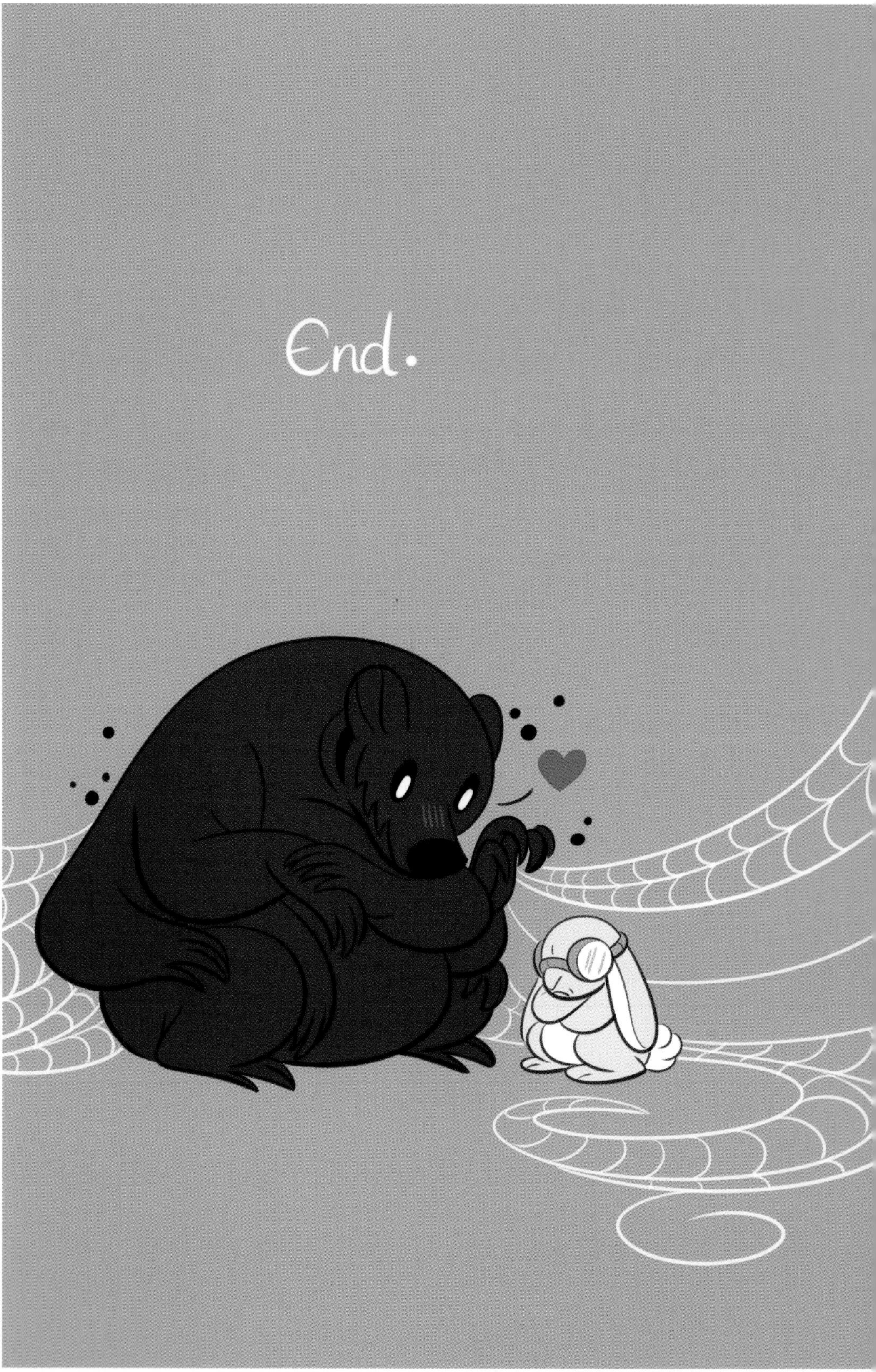
End.

How to Make A Comic Page
From Scribbles to Finished Artwork

If you're an aspiring comic artist or just curious, here's how I usually go about making a comic page. Remember though, there's no one way to do it and as long as you manage to get a page finished I'd count that as a win...even if your own method takes 50 different steps and frequent breaks to cry.

-Sam

Step 1:
Scribbling while Scripting

When I'm writing out the script for a comic I'll often do VERY loose scribbles for page layout ideas at the same time. This is to check that what I'm writing will make sense visually. I don't have an image to show you for this stage because it wouldn't look like anything but squiggly lines to anyone but me.

That said, here are some thumbnails that I drew up for the first part of this book! (They are slightly nicer than scribbles.)

Step 2:
Sketch

Once the script is done, I read through the descriptions and make a rough sketch, paying attention to the big shapes and poses. When I'm happy with that, I'll sometimes go back over objects and characters to refine details, or sometimes I'll leave that until the inking stage for more organic shapes like hair or clothing. If I'm drawing a complicated object that I feel less confident in, then I'll take much more time to get the details and perspective right at the sketching stage. I also don't worry much about line weight or making 'pretty' drawings at this stage, it's more about communicating the story clearly.

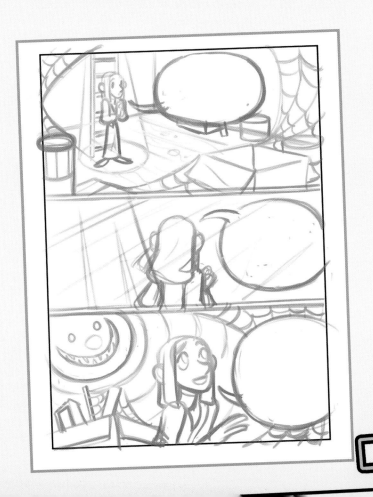

Step 3:
Inks

Here is when I start thinking more about line quality and good shape design. I'll pay attention to keeping the characters looking 'on model' and flesh out any details that I left vague at the sketch stage. You can see I added quite a few background object details at the inking stage. I try to keep a good balance of black and white on the page and see if spots of pure black can enhance the storytelling. In this case, since Clarion's in a big creepy basement, leaving the back wall completely in shadow and undefined helps reinforce that feeling. Notice that the background behind the speech bubbles is also drawn in even though you won't see most of it in the final image, this gives the letterer more options when they come to add the speech balloons and text.

Step 4:
Flat Colors

I spend quite a long time figuring out the basic colors that I want on the page. I think about what characters or objects I want the reader's eye to go to first and try to place the brighter or more saturated colors there. With this page the choices were a little easier since the basement is dark–it made sense for most of the objects to be the same dark blue. However, even in a brightly lit scene, it might still be a good idea to have background elements one color to keep things from looking too busy on the page and to keep the focus on your characters.

Step 5:
Touch Ups &
Smaller Color Details

At this stage I will add some light gradients or highlights and alter any shapes that I feel aren't quite working the way I want. I've added more detail to the Bugbear's shadowy grin to make it creepier and also removed some of the line work in the very bright area by the ladder in the first panel. If something looks a bit off to me or didn't come out quite as I wanted but I know the reader will understand it, I will leave it be and just challenge myself to draw it better next time. Comics is more about story flow than beautiful perfect pages to me...but every artist has their own balancing point and only drawing many, many pages will allow you to find where you are comfortable saying a page is 'done'.

Step 6:
The final page with letters!

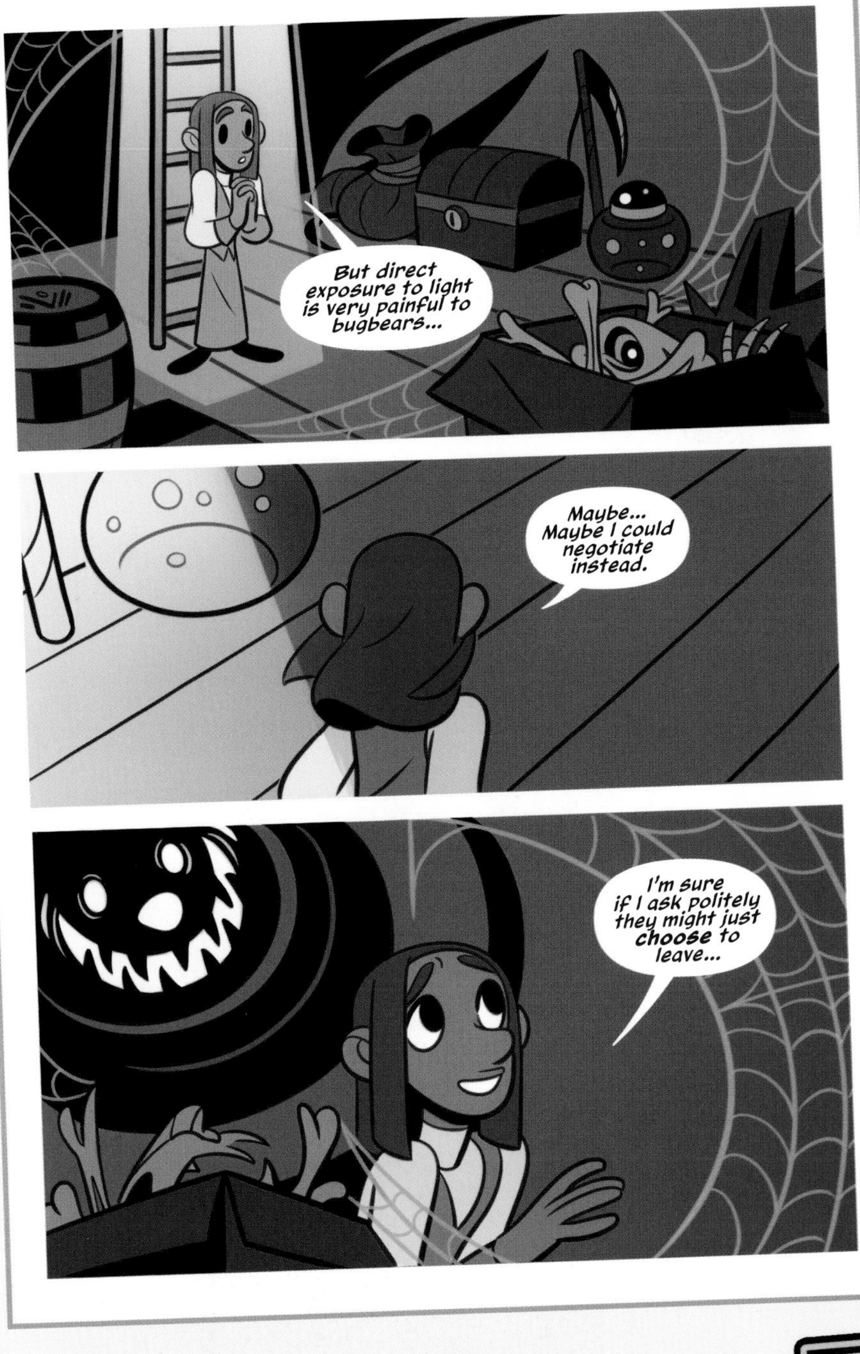
But direct exposure to light is very painful to bugbears...
Maybe... Maybe I could negotiate instead.
I'm sure if I ask politely they might just choose to leave...

So on that note, why don't you go and try to draw some!

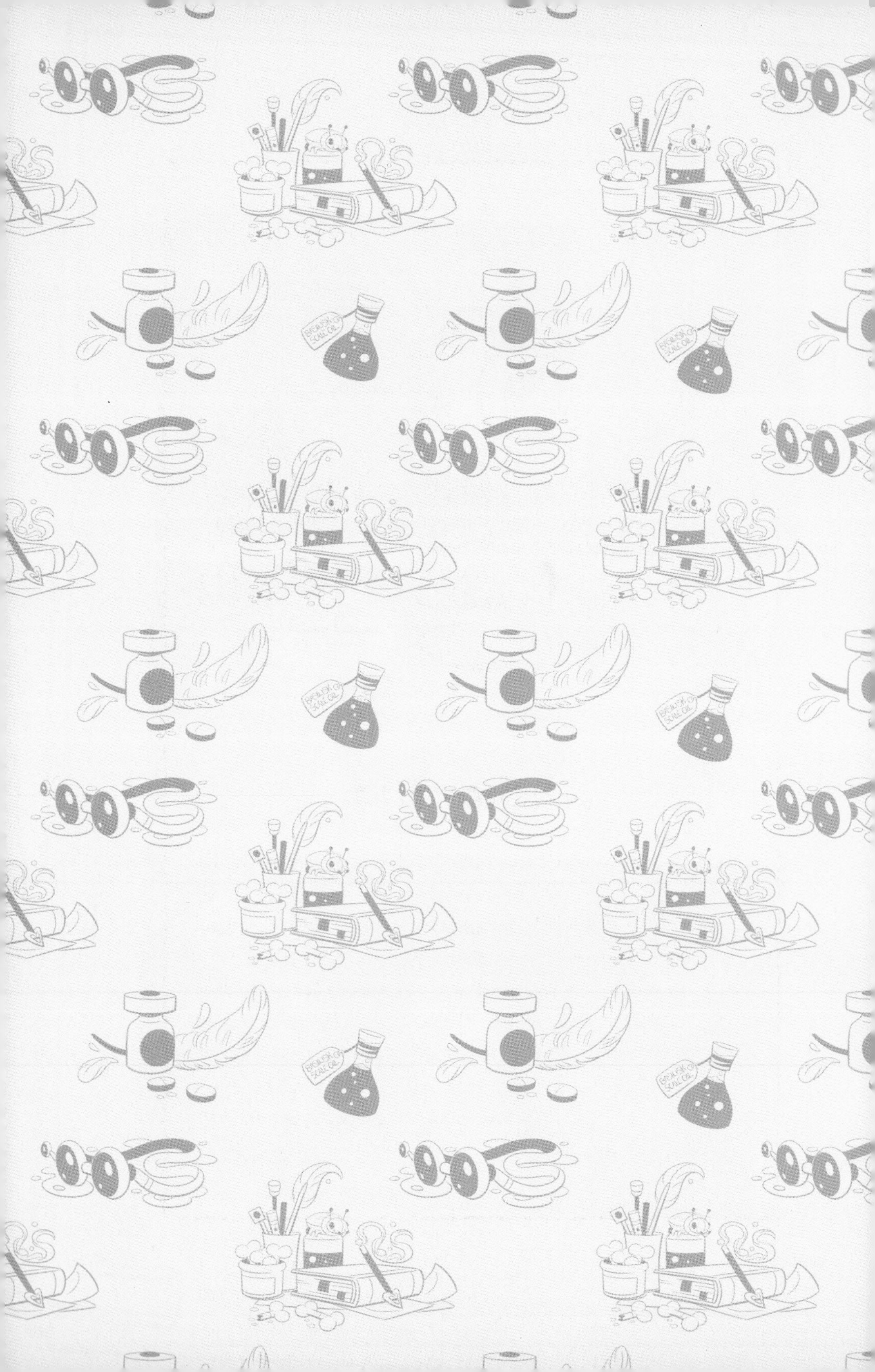
BASILISK SCALE OIL

Author Bio

Sam Davies is an illustrator and comic artist living somewhere in the UK countryside, probably near some ducks. She's best known for her online silent all-ages comics series *Stutterhug* which currently has over 160 strips and will probably keep going until someone stops her. If you meet her in person, she likes talking about ghost stories and animal species that don't exist. *Hex Vet: Witches in Training* is her first graphic novel and she hopes you have a good time reading it.

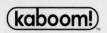